THE WEANING HILL

JOE EDD MORRIS

Black Rose Writing | Texas

ISBN: 978-1-68513-627-7 (Paperback); 978-1-68513-657-4 (Hardcover)
LIBRARY OF CONGRESS CONTROL NUMBER: 2025934572
PUBLISHED BY BLACK ROSE WRITING
www.blackrosewriting.com

Printed in the United States of America
Suggested Retail Price (SRP) $18.95 (Paperback); $25.95 (Hardcover)

The Weaning Hill is printed in Garamond Premier Pro

*As a planet-friendly publisher, Black Rose Writing does its best to eliminate unnecessary waste to reduce paper usage and energy costs, while never compromising the reading experience. As a result, the final word count vs. page count may not meet common expectations.

"When the child has grown big and must be weaned, the mother
virginally hides her breast, so the child has no more a mother.
Happy the child which did not in another way lose its mother."
—Søren Kierkegaard
Fear and Trembling

"Blow on the coal of the heart ...
Blow on the coal of the heart.
And we'll see by and by ..."
—Archibald MacLeish
J.B

THE
WEANING
HILL

PART ONE

1

Hap and Liz

He leaned on the ax, wiped his brow and looked back at the house on top of the hill, its tin roof an orange sheet of fire, its smokeless chimney a dark notch in the clear late Indian summer sky.

Don't it look good, he thought, all new and shiny. No more leaks. They won't go cold this winter neither.

He cupped his hand over his eyes and glanced across the highway and wide bottom below where the sun was leaving long shadows then followed the bare slopes from the house into thick woods that walled the place off from the rest of the world. Their color looked too pretty to be dying, but the leaves would be gone soon, wrenched from their branches in the winter storm that was surely coming. Any time it got this warm in November, look out, his daddy had said, a snowstorm was just around the corner. North Mississippi's red-clay hills hadn't seen one of those in a while, not one he could remember in his twenty-nine years. That may have been the last, when he was born, winter of '42. His mother said it was snowing when he came into the world. He was ready for any storm.

· · ·

She stood and watched him through the kitchen window as she nursed the baby. He picked up the ax and chainsaw and began walking from the wood stack toward the house, one foot loping in front of the other, his face tilted at the sky like he didn't have a care in the world. She needed to look away but kept her eyes on him. In his red shirt and new hunting vest and new leather boots, he didn't look like he'd been working. But she'd never really seen him work, not real work anyway, not farm work.

As he came closer, she could see the pinkish flush on his face, the tiny spikes his sandy hair made across his forehead, the cowlick sticking up in back like a wild sprout. He'd sweated a little. She'd give him that. But nothing else about him had changed. He looked as boyish and contented as the day she married him, ten years ago almost to the day. She caught the side of her lip in her teeth and bit down, for strength. She had to tell him today. She couldn't wait any longer.

She turned and walked through the dining room toward the front porch and stopped in the living room. In the mantel mirror, she watched the tiny movements of the baby's head beneath her blouse. The image brought some comfort, reminded her of the good mother she was, and had been. But when she looked at the photos in the room, she remembered too much. Fairest of the Fair, Homecoming Queen, Miss Hatchie High—earned all those titles the year they married. Her face was pretty then. She moved her hand over the hollows beneath her eyes. Her cheeks were full then. She touched at the gray along her temples. Her hair black and shiny, then. She bought new clothes, then, two sizes smaller. People looked, then. She was happy, then. That was going to change.

She stepped closer to the mirror. She moved her mouth and puffed her cheeks, but they wouldn't go away, the fine hair-like creases that drew her face toward her chin. Using her fingers she stretched the skin on each side of her mouth, just to see. Yep. And they weren't smile lines. She ran her hand over her hair, tucked loose strands on the side back into place and piled the ponytail up on top. Maybe she should just cut it or wear it in a bun. She looked into her eyes, which helped. She'd lost nothing there. They were as hazel and bright as ever, but even they couldn't take away the tired that hung on her. He'd never understand that. He, who since their marriage, had not once said thank you or shown any appreciation for her housework and mothering and keeping everything in order, like they were all painless duties ordained and instituted by God. He, who lay on the couch every evening watching television, never lifting a finger, asking her to bring him popcorn, brew him coffee, change the channels, which she did, never complaining. He, who'd been home laid off temporarily from the factory two weeks, and the only thing he'd contributed, a stack of wood and walking toward her now with that look on his face like he'd cleared a lower forty single-handed. Holding those thoughts, she turned and walked away.

•   •   •

She'll be proud, he thought, as he neared the house. Five cords finally cut and stacked. She'll smile when she comes out and sees them. They'll last all winter.

"Lizzie, honey," he hollered. "Come out on the porch. Got something to show you. Ruthie, you and Kevin come too." They were only nine and eight, but they'd appreciate this.

She walked onto the front porch with the baby in the crook of her arm. Her blouse was unbuttoned, and he could see a white mound of breast where the baby was nursing. The children followed, the screen door slapping shut behind them. The dog on the front step pushed up, wheeled then plopped down again and curled back into his nap. The children clung tightly to their mother's skirt. They looked scared. His hollering had probably done that. They didn't like it when anybody hollered.

He stopped at the end of the porch and pointed the ax handle toward the stacked wood. "Now don't that look good?"

She said nothing and was not smiling. Neither were the children. He dropped the ax and chainsaw to the ground. He turned and looked at the ricks of wood for a moment then back at her and the children.

"That's five cords, stacked neat as a made bed. I worked hard on 'em. You can get 'em easy now, and they won't roll on you when you pull one."

She was still silent. Her mouth stretched a little, tugged slightly in the corners as she breathed deeply. He'd pull it on out into a smile. "With the new roof and insulation and all, you and the little ones won't get wet or cold this winter." She just stood there looking at him, a cold, hard look on her face, not even close to a smile.

•   •   •

She needed to be mad when she told him. Toward this moment she'd worked her anger. For days, she'd fought through the junk heap of memory—ten years' worth—and dragged out every hardship and pain he'd inflicted upon her, whipped herself into the maddest heat ever till there was nothing he could do or say that would cool her down.

From beneath her blouse, tiny slurping noises. Around her hips, the pressure of her children's heads and hands tight against her, their bodies still as if someone had painted them onto her. When it was over, these would steady her, keep her on track.

"Ruthie, you and Kevin go in the back and play," she said. "Your daddy and I have to talk."

"We gotta *what*?" he said.

The children whimpered, clutching her tighter.

She raised her voice. "Go on now. Do as I say, before you get a whipping." The baby began crying as they scampered off the end of the porch and disappeared around the corner of the house. With careful fingers, she adjusted the baby's head against her breast and gently guided its mouth back to her nipple, then looked at him. "Hap, the kids and I are going to Mama's."

His head snapped. Not at what she said. Going to her parents was not unusual. But the way she said it, like something thrown at him. "You *what*?"

"You heard me. The kids and I are going to Mama's, and not just for overnight either."

"You gotta be ... what the hell?"

"I'm leaving you." She surprised herself. Like an old festered sore that needed no help bursting, the words popped out.

His strength drained through his legs like a plug had been pulled. She watched as he turned green, like he was going to be sick, his eyes searching her face in disbelief. But her eyes were cold and unblinking.

"You can't." He struggled for another breath. "You can't give it up, just like that."

"It isn't *our* place, Hap. It belongs to *your* family. Always has. Always will and—"

"Daddy give it to us, Lizzie. Told us we could have it. Nothing wrong with that."

She stared at the self-pitying face turned up at her and felt another onrush of anger. "*Loaned*, Hap. He *loaned* it to us, just like he did your brothers and sisters and their families until they could get their own places. A thirty-acre farm that hasn't grown anything in over twenty years. People make fun of it. They call it 'the weaning hill.' I want my place, one I can call my own, so when folks look at it they'll see rows of beans and a stand of corn and a garden to fill the freezer and say, 'There's the Pasley place.'"

He leapt onto the porch and grabbed her shoulders. "We'll get our own place, honey. Gimme some time. Factory just laid us off two weeks. Start back Monday. Won't be long 'fore I can make an offer on the old Pullen place."

She snapped her shoulders free and stepped back. The baby let out a little cry until his mouth quickly found its place again.

"New roof sounds like we'll be here a while. You've been dangling the Pullen place in front of me long enough. Nothing's been the same around here since that factory came to town. Farms going to pot. Land going to weeds. Government paying folks not to plant. Husbands leaving work and going to the Jottem Down or Ruby's Place, drinking beer, playing pool, coming in all hours of the night. I want a place of my own and a man that goes with it, a plot of land that holds the man to it, like the good Lord meant it to be."

She'd hit below the belt. He threw a finger in her face. "I ain't been to those joints in a long time. Ain't drank any neither, not since the revival last fall."

His rededication. She knew she'd live to see the day it'd be thrown up in her face.

His finger was shaking but he kept it on her. "And if it wadn't for the factory, some of us'd be on food stamps or going hungry. Hadn't none of my family ever gone on welfare."

She reached up with the hand not holding the baby and brushed the finger in her face aside. "Just what would you do if the factory shut down? All you've got is thirty acres of this hill and those woods." She pointed toward them and took a step closer. "What're you going to do with the Pullen place? Farm? You've never farmed a day in your life, Hap Pasley. You went straight from high school to that factory, like all the rest of them."

She was rocking the baby and talking mad at the same time. A bird swooped in under the eave of the porch, fluttered around a nest then flew off.

"I want to smell fresh cut hay and the sweetness of land that's been broken open by a plow. I want a man working the land so his children can see him and be proud of him, see him so one day they'll know what to do with their lives. I want to stand with my man and watch plants and calves grow and put up a garden in the fall and feel proud that we did it all, that the money we pay our bills with didn't come from somebody wearing a suit living up North who doesn't give a damn about people's lives down here. And I intend to get it. The kids and I are leaving. And that's that."

Her face was red. The veins in her forehead bulged. He was drowning, and she was the only thing he could grab. He sank to his knees and pressed his head between her legs. "But you can't, Lizzie, you just can't. I love you. I love you. I can't live without you. Please don't go. Please ... please ... "

She looked down at the crumpled body groveling at her feet, blubbering like a baby, a thing much less than a man, hardly more than a child. "You can live without me. It's this hill you can't live without," she said, as though the words were the last thing she could hit him with. But she wasn't through. "I've already packed and called daddy. He's on his way." She nodded toward the macadam highway in the distance, at the end of a long, gutted dirt road that crooked its way to the house. "Now, quit acting like a two-year old. You'll make the baby cry."

She twisted from his grasp and walked away. The baby began crying. The dog raised again and lumbered from the steps to a safer spot under the house.

She returned to the front bedroom, laid the baby on the bed and hurriedly placed pillows around him. She tried to avoid looking at anything that reminded her of happier times—pictures on the wall, wedding presents, the carnival bear in the corner he'd won for her at the last fair. But the room was too full of them, of her and him. Quickly, she began changing clothes and made herself think of her new life.

He was still on his knees on the warped planking of the porch. All he saw were her legs disappearing through the door. His mind spun back through the pain and shock to the time he'd first really noticed her, sitting in church on the same pew where he sat, tanned legs and dainty feet rising from shiny black heels that sent a warm rush through him and caused him to check out the rest of her. He thought of last night and countless others, the soft touch of her legs and ankles and feet against his, the final signal, as sure and trustworthy as his mother's goodnight kiss when he was a child, that all was well, and would be, that he could go to sleep. His thoughts jolted forward in time, to Hap Pasley alone in a cold bed and empty house. He bent over and cried at the floor. Wrapped in his own arms, he rocked, tried to smother his hurt in his lap. The children mustn't hear.

• • •

He somehow reached that point where crying, sooner or later, stops. Something pulled him up. It couldn't have been himself. He was too weak. Yet, he was standing, gazing westward from the porch where she liked to sit and rock each evening and watch the long river bottom beyond the highway disappear after first dark. He'd sit and rock with her. He never gained the peace she did from that dusky view. He drew his from her.

He sat on the top step, let his eyes dry and rest. Soon, he'd have to look at the children. In front of him a spider was drawing a line from the ceiling. By its color and shape it looked dangerous, something he knew to respect. He spread his legs to let it pass, watched to see if it would make it to the step, wondering how the thin thread held something so much bigger, remembering hearing somewhere that the quicker and longer the thread is drawn out, the stronger it becomes.

An eighteen-wheeler droned along the highway and beyond the sun hung above the horizon where a cloud of copper-colored dust trailed a tractor. Billy Ray was plowing his field, turning under dry cornstalks, working as long as daylight would allow. Billy Ray Rather. He lived on a hundred-acre farm across the highway. A highway that sliced through the land dividing red clay hills from fertile bottom land, poor farmers from rich farmers, those who fought just to hang on to the land and those who could buy more. A byway that got to be called a highway, way back in time, for that very same reason—not for where it went but for what it divided.

He and Billy Ray had grown up together. Gone to school together, been baptized together. They graduated together and married and, with only a highway and acreage between them, drifted apart. Then Billy Ray's wife died. That was two years ago. He came often to their house for meals; even after they both quit insisting. Lizzie cooked new recipes and made a fuss about it all. He'd never given it much thought. Now he wondered what she did during the day with him at work and the children in school and just the baby to take care of and looking fresh as spring sitting in her rocker on the porch when he came home—but not the first touch of makeup while he'd been home laid off for two weeks.

Like a fire after the wood shifts, a blaze flared inside him. "By God, so that's it." He barely felt a sticky spider strand across his hand as he jumped up and headed for the front door. He caught himself midway and stopped, listened, made sure he could hear the children's voices in the backyard.

The screen door slapped against the wall and hit him in the back on his way in. He sidestepped suitcases in the entrance and stumbled toward her where she stood looking in the mirror over the mantel, adjusting her hair. She had wound it into a bun on top of her head. She had changed clothes, too, into a yellow dress and hose and low black pumps, like she was going somewhere important.

"Billy Ray Rather!"

"What?" She was half turned, her head tucked downward as she opened a bobby pin with her teeth.

"Billy ... Ray ... Rather." He said the words slowly this time, louder, then waited.

She speared the knot of hair with the bobby pin and spun completely around. Her eyes glared at him like an animal's suddenly spotlighted. Her chest heaved. She leaned an elbow on the mantel and propped her other hand on her hip. "I don't know what you're talking about."

Her eyes hit him waist-high at his buckle, and he spotted a nervous twitch in the side of her mouth to match the twitch in the hand hanging from the mantel, guilt dripping from her like she was melting.

"You don't need to say no more. I think I know what you been—Godalmighty!"

He slapped his hand to his leg and hopped on one foot.

"I swear, Hap," she let out a hollow laugh, "if you don't beat all."

"Damn spider. It bit me." He looked first at the black wad on the floor then at a small red spot on his leg where swelling had already begun. "I've got to put something on it. Think it was a black widow. Quick. What'll I do?"

Neither had heard the car pull up in front, so when the horn honked, they froze.

"I don't know," she said. "Daddy's here. I've got to get the baby and kids."

She left him holding his leg, but another pain surged through him, its center in the bottom of his throat. Limping, he followed her down the hallway, his hand still clutching his leg.

"Lizzie. Lizzie, wait. I didn't mean it that hard. We can talk about it."

She ignored him and called out the names of the children, and grabbing their coats from the hat tree in the hall.

Giggling and scuffling, Kevin and Ruthie spilled through the back door, one pulling on the other.

They came suddenly, tumbling through his head like photos upturned from a box. Memories. First cries and laughter, first birthdays, first bicycles. Trips to the zoo in Memphis and Liberty Land and Sunday picnics in the park, Christmas mornings and school plays and nighttime prayers and little warm bodies piling playfully into bed on top of them in the mornings. Like the best parts of a movie, they fell, flicking, then buried him in an avalanche of grief as the children rushed into his arms, and he felt the smoothness of their cheeks on his and the smell of their clean skin and the message of their little arms tight around his neck and all he could do was tremble and breathe words he couldn't say but finally managed: "Daddy loves you," over and over. Then they were gone, running toward the front door hollering, "Granddaddy! Granddaddy!" And he heard the screen door slam and knew they were in another world of care, happy again.

Unstoppable streams burned his cheeks as he stood and looked at her and saw, for the first time, a glimmer of hope. Her mouth quivered. Tears gathered in the corners of her eyes.

•   •   •

Don't weaken now, she told herself. *Be strong, Lizzie, be strong.* She felt an old habit pushing but she pulled back from hugging him and placed a hand instead on his arm and squeezed.

"I'll call later," she said, her voice quieter, softer. "You'll be able to see the children. Don't worry about that. I'm not trying to take them from you. This is something I need to do, for me."

•   •   •

For me, he thought. What about the children? What about him? What about family and home and keeping that together?

She walked past him toward their bedroom at the front of the house. He followed her up the narrow hallway, watched her unbroken, even movement. Though thinner than when they married, her body attracted him more than ever, its shape visible beneath her dress in the last level rays of sunlight that framed her in the front door, just for a moment, before she turned.

In the shadows of the room, the baby lay on the bed between two pillows, his fists clenched, his brow furrowed, like a tiny soldier finished with battle. She stood back to let his father do what he needed to do. He slipped his hands under the cotton blanket where the little feet oared and lifted him up close, close enough to feel his breath coming in little puffs from his open mouth and smell his sweet powder. *He won't remember*, he thought. *Thank the good Lord, he won't remember.* He kissed the baby lightly on the cheek and handed him to her.

He walked with her to the porch and another strategy of hope came to him. Her family's church meant everything, the world, to them. They wouldn't miss church if tornado warnings were out. Because of church, there'd never been a divorce in their family; they were not allowed. Liz just needed a chance to talk it over with them.

He opened the front door for her.

Her father, a large white-haired man, had already taken the suitcases to the bottomed-out Ford that might make it another year. He moved with the deliberate and careful slowness of his eighty years. When they stepped through the screen door onto the porch, he stood propped in the open door of the car, bent over watching the children play in the backseat, as if he wanted to see nothing else in this world at that moment.

"Mr. Turpin?" Hap called out. They'd always been close. He felt a part of her family, was always warmly received. Her father would at least listen to his side, hear him out.

Her father glanced up and flipped a hand dangling over the door frame. "Hiddy, Hap. Looks like a big'un moving in over yonder." He pointed toward the west where a wall of dark clouds stretched across the sky. "See you got your wood cut in time," smiling as he said it.

He probably doesn't even know, Hap thought. The men usually didn't. "Yessir. Five cords."

"Five cords you say. That oughtta last a man a winter."

"Yessir. Ought to." He wanted to say more but now was not the time. Keeping a hand on her elbow, he helped her down the steps, leaned over to kiss her, but she quickly shifted the baby to that side and spoke hurriedly.

"We'll be at Mama and Daddy's. Call when you need to. She spoke to the children who had disappeared to the floor of the car. Sit up and wave goodbye to your daddy." They popped up and waved, half-smiling, eager to go back to playing.

2

Hap

He stood at the edge of the porch and watched the beam from the headlights bounce around the curves of the dirt drive then turn onto the highway. He raised his hand and waved. The kids were waving through the rear window. Even if he couldn't see them, he knew they were. He couldn't see them, but he knew they were. They always did. He hoped they saw him, that she did too. She couldn't have stopped loving him just like that. She was looking even if she wasn't waving. She couldn't leave without looking back. Nobody could do that, live on a place ten years and not look back. The kids would make her do that. "Mommy, look at Daddy and wave," they were telling her. They were doing that. They wouldn't let her forget their daddy, he prayed.

He kept watching and waving until they were out of sight, then it struck him, up high, around his eyes and throat before sinking through him like a lead weight in quicksand, a slow shock that was just beginning, a fear spreading through him.

He looked back across the bottom. Dusk lay over the land, a thin red line beneath purple rolls of clouds that pushed down on the swollen sun, squeezing it out of the sky, pressing it toward another side of the world, into another tomorrow somewhere far away. Above all that, clear heavens with a quarter moon and evening star but nothing else. The only moving thing he could see, the lights of Billy Ray's tractor. He was still at work, plowing.

He rammed his fist against the wall then walked inside. A stiff, cool breeze followed, reminding him to close the door. The house was quiet, quieter than quiet. He heard sounds he'd never heard before. Creaks in the walls and floors. Whispers around the windows. The ticking of the grandfather clock down the hallway. Chimneyswifts flapping in the flue. The empty fireplace breathing the smell of old fires. He'd never been alone. Someone had always been there. A mother. A father. Brothers and sisters. A wife. Children. A heaviness he couldn't name fell upon him, through him. He sat on the edge of the sofa in the living room and tried a prayer. Not one that thanked or blessed. He couldn't get that far. But one that asked *Why?* Over and over and over and the crying started again, deep, hammering in his stomach. He lay down on the hard cushions and closed his eyes, his hands cold on his face, his thoughts drowning, and slipped into an uneasy asleep.

An ache gnawed in his leg. He shook and reached for covers that weren't there. His eyes opened to strange darkness, strange shadows. A splash of light from a hallway. A mirror. Mantel. Fireplace. Rug. His eyes began to adjust. The shapes of home drove the pain through him again, and he wanted to return to the oblivion of sleep. The cold braced him instead and he sat up. He needed to build a fire and treat his wound.

Outside, the wind was brisk and chilling. He thought about the clouds rolling in and what his father had said about winter storms and how smart his father was and how much he needed him now. He walked to the cords of wood he'd just cut and lifted four logs from the top of a stack that never moved. He'd told her right. He'd stacked them that good.

He opened the front door and something moved, nudged against his legs. It was Homer, his dog, ready to come in for the night. A moment of comfort, something needing him. He took several sticks from the kindling box and criss-crossed them over the grate then added the logs. He lit a stove match to the newspaper he'd wadded under the grate. Homer lay on the rug beside him, watching for the umpteenth time, but his large, brown eyes wide and shimmering like it was the first. In a short while the kindling caught, crackling and popping, sending short yellow flames licking through the logs like thirst.

He grabbed the flashlight they always kept by the bed and went again into the night air. At the rear of the house, where the back porch was higher off the ground, he peered into the darkness. Holding tightly to the flashlight, he crawled on his elbows and knees, like a soldier on a battlefield, through cobwebs and dancing crickets, through the smell of damp decay and old dirt to the brick piling where he remembered burying it over a year ago. With anxious bare hands, he clawed the ground, his fingers palpating the object's shape, working it back and forth until the fifth of Early Times came loose and he pulled it from its fungal crypt. He shook off the dirt and unscrewed the top and took a swallow. Part of the pain burned away so he took another, longer than the first, felt the fire all the way to his stomach. He set the flashlight on the ground so the beam would hit his leg and poured a stream over a raised red welt the size of a half-dollar. He gritted his teeth as the alcohol did its job. She'd have known better what to do.

He reentered the house and removed an ice tray from the freezer compartment. He'd seen her do it a million times, bend the plastic tray and punch it with her thumbs. He tried. Cubes slid everywhere across the countertop. Some hit the floor and slipped away, invisible on the white tile. "Shit." He grabbed the ones on the counter, the ones he could see, then realized he didn't have a glass. Where'd she keep them? He searched wildly, throwing open overhead cabinets. The ice was burning his hands. Glasses, finally. "Shit," again. "Glasses, finally. He threw the melting cubes into the glass. His hands were trembling. He thought it was because he hadn't eaten, or maybe they were just cold. A sick feeling churned in his stomach. The bottle shook in his hand as he poured. He watched and listened as the ice crackled to the touch of the golden brown liquid. A strong, sweet smell floated into the air, a smell of other times, other places.

He took the bottle and glass and walked to the couch. The fire was blazing. Homer was asleep, snoring. He thought of turning on the television, but that would only bring back memories, sad ones. They always watched it together in the evenings after the children were in bed. He on the couch. She knitting in the chair at the end. Sometimes, she sitting beside him. She getting him his popcorn, bringing him his coffee. She just being there, making everything all right. She. She was gone. He stared at the flames. *She.*

By the higher tone of the singing around the windows, he could tell the wind was picking up. The ice rattled in the glass like it was in the wind, and he raised it to his mouth. The ice rattled more. He gripped the glass with both hands, but it kept shaking. Whiskey sloshed over the rim, dousing his front and lap. "Shit fire! What the hell's going on. Can't even hold a damn glass." He stood up and threw the glass into the fireplace where it popped and shattered like a light bulb and the fire flared. Homer leaped up as if he'd heard gun shot, turned his head around like he was waiting for a kick, then lay down and returned to his dream.

"By damn, I'm gonna drink." He grabbed the bottle and clutched it with both hands, sucked down several deep swigs and planted it between his legs trying to ignore the pain in his leg. *It'll go away 'fore long*, he thought. *Maybe it wadn't a black widow.*

He leaned back in the couch, and his eyes roamed the house. Little was his or hers, so precious few things they'd bought with their own money that they could call theirs. The television. The vanity. Bedroom furniture. Appliances. Even most of the clothes. Hand-me-downs, either there when they moved in or given to them by his parents.

A sharp pain ripped upward from his stomach. At first he thought it was the whiskey. But whiskey'd never done that. A spasm followed, like a cramp. He sucked on the bottle again, pumping down more relief. His head dizzied, and his thoughts returned, swirled around her. She wanted a man. "By damn, I'll show her what a man is," he said to himself. He stood up. "I'll show her and him, Billy Ray Rather, so-called friend, family breaker. I'll show ever'body." He sat again and glared at the fire, lifted the bottle to his lips occasionally for quick swills. "I'll show ever'body."

A warmness, like sunlight after a long cloud, spread across his face. His thoughts drifted.

A strange feeling began to work his thinking. Thoughts ran loose in his head. He was past the point where one feeling ended and another began. His insides were a wild river that needed banks and some place to empty. The spasms in his stomach came closer together and harder, and his hands could hardly bring the bottle to his mouth. The walls of the room swam, and the floor rushed toward him as he stood up. He made his way to the door and onto the porch, Homer right behind him. The fresh air would make him feel better.

The wind blew colder in strong gusts that smelled of rain. He stood on the porch, strained his eyes, and blinked. It couldn't be, he thought. He strained and blinked again. By damn, it was. Headlights and taillights crawled along the highway, and beyond them, another light, moving slower. Billy Ray was still at it. "I'll give that sombitch somethin' to look at."

His feet clomped on patches of light along the porch. He stumbled to the end and jumped into blackness. The ground came up hard on his face, but the bottle was still in his hand. He poured where he guessed his mouth was. A stream of fire hit the back of his throat then stopped. "Shit!" He hurled the bottle against the side of the house where it made a dull clunk. He scrambled around in the dark of the yard.

"Sombitch's out here somewhere."

A hand caught the sharp teeth of the chainsaw and fumbled its way back to the handle. He struggled to his feet. The machine's weight pulled him forward toward the porch and uprighted him when he slammed against it.

"Damn porch."

His fingers found the handle on the crank cord, and he gave a quick yank. The saw roared like a plane diving out of the pitch-dark sky. He braced his elbows against his sides and lifted the howling saw into the air like it was a wild animal in a harness and brought it down hard against the corner post of the porch, severing it like a sapling.

"Take that, you mother. She won't have to look at you no more. I won't neither." He leaned against the porch and scooted along its edge to the next post. The circling teeth zipped through it and the ceiling sagged with a loud crunch. When he moved to cut the next post, the saw sputtered and died and he heaved it into the dark.

He clambered up the front steps that swam beneath his feet and yelled at the door handle that danced around his hands. "Stay still, dammit," then hurled his body through the screen door. He picked himself up from the floor and stumbled toward the hallway, ricocheting off the walls and into the children's room. He pulled at drawers and closets, tossed clothes onto the bed, gathered the spread, knotted it and dragged the bundle through the house onto the porch and down the steps into the yard. He scrambled back up the steps into the house and the front bedroom, their room. He pulled pictures from the wall his screaming thoughts told him to save then stumbled to the gun case in the hall. "This'll do it. This here'll end this shit." He crashed his fist through the glass and grabbed the double-barreled shotgun he always kept loaded. "Die, sombitch. Die."

He could go now to Billy Ray's, and was on his way toward the door when he looked at the fireplace. "Ain't through yet." He stopped to think how to do it. The spasm hit his stomach again. A vomit lump climbed his throat and his body shook. He dropped the pictures and shotgun onto the couch and faltered toward the fireplace. Tiny blue-yellow flames flickered over a bed of orange coals. He grabbed the shovel from the rack and began scooping live coals, slinging them around the room until he was out of breath. Small red eyes stared at him from the dark hearth. Gotta get out now, he thought. He found the shotgun and pictures on the couch and staggered onto the porch into the yard. His knees collapsed onto the hard ground next to the bundle of clothes and he began throwing up. His insides spewed out of his mouth until there was nothing left, and his body jerked in dry spasms, leaving him limp when it finally stopped.

He looked up at the house. The lights were still on, as though a family was still inside. The only smoke he could see, a thin wisp curling from the chimney. He began beating his fists on the ground then against the sides of his head, bawling, "Can't even burn a house down, dammit. Can't even burn … a house … down."

He reached for the shotgun and used it to push himself up.

"But by damn … there's one damn thing … I can do."

He tucked a handful of pictures under his arm and was still crying as he pitched down the road toward the highway, tears warping his eyes that could still see a light, distorted and magnified, moving slowly in the distance.

3

Liz

The car lurched and rocked down the rutted drive. Like a river of glowing coals, the clouds stretched endlessly across the dimming sky. She was not going to look back and was afraid to look ahead across the highway, so when she glanced out the window, her eyes caught the jarred shadow of the house in the side view mirror.

Her father waited until he had made the turn from the dirt lane onto the highway before he spoke.

"Looks like Billy Ray's working way overtime tonight." He gave a nervous cough and cleared his throat. "Guess he's trying to finish that field 'fore that storm gets here the weatherman's predicting."

"Yessir. Guess so." She rarely lied to her father. Billy Ray told her he'd be there for moral support, just for her to see, to remind her, probably to keep her from forgetting as well. She tried to smother the thought, but it slid downward, along with her heart, and beat hard in her stomach. She pulled the baby closer to her breasts and nudged its head into the crook of her shoulder, for her own comfort as much as the baby's. Beyond the bright shimmering edges of the headlights, the darkening land parted and rushed around them with the wind, like an airy ocean taking them into its undertow. Sudden sharp gusts shook and veered the car at times, causing her to fumble for something to hold on to. A cold handle on the door.

Her father's thick hands wrapped the steering wheel as though it belonged to a tractor, and as hard to steer. His eyes stapled the dotted center line of the road, but she felt them hitting her. For the next few miles his silence penetrated her like a search light, focused, steady. The kids were playing some quiet and mysterious game on the floor of the backseat, withdrawn into a world they could control. When her father finally spoke, she jumped.

"You sure 'bout this, Sis?"

It was the same question he'd asked when she told him she was going to marry Hap Pasley. Then she was sure. There was no question. He was caring, thoughtful and attentive. The drinking hadn't been a problem. A few beers with friends after fishing or hunting. He'd attempted two poems and sent them to her. The fact they half-rhymed and half-made sense didn't matter. They revealed a sensitive side of manhood she'd never known, a tenderness that surprised, ambushed her. They dated off and on and eventually went steady their senior year. She held onto her virginity like she'd promised her mother, and God, until the urge and the heat, the pulsing ache, was too much. So, when he told her he had the job at the new shirt factory upon graduation and the house on the hill with thirty acres, she was sure. It didn't matter she was valedictorian and had a scholarship. It didn't matter she wasn't going to college and might never be a nurse, that the man who proposed to her barely passed his last two years of high school, never went out for sports, but would have lettered in pool, every year were it offered. Nothing mattered. There was no question. She couldn't wait. They were married the day after graduation and spent their honeymoon at the Peabody in Memphis where they sat and watched the ducks swim around the huge lobby fountain and clinked glasses filled with golden champagne and giggled and smiled for the roving black photographer who gave them the picture she left hanging on the wall. There was a lot she could leave behind, and did. But these memories played now on her mind, like temptations. She knew she had to answer her father.

"I think so."

He said nothing, which was not unusual, but he was probably protecting the children. His silence continued, adding more to her uncertainty. In the faint light of the dashboard dials, the features of his face tapered into a stiff grimness that seemed to lodge in his chin and pull his head downward. She thought of his age and how all this would affect him and her mother. Both were in their mid-seventies, the sunset years, the best ones of their lives. They knew she was unhappy. She had to trust they'd understand. Her thoughts traveled ahead, along the edges of a future she'd dreamed about. They slid over Billy Ray's strong face and voice and words and firm body and a family on a farm like her father and brothers, but always came back to Hap, and she tried to work her anger again, which helped. If she could just stay mad. If he just hadn't rededicated his life and quit drinking. She found herself resenting conversions she once cried over with joy. It was hard enough staying mad at somebody she once worshipped, who was struggling to climb back onto that pedestal, and easier to love somebody she now worshipped, and harder still to make it all fit somehow into her conscience.

"Kids seem okay," her father said in a low voice that rose slightly on the last syllable.

She studied that for a moment, whether he was stating or asking, then answered him. "Yes. They're doing fine."

Her father and mother were not the types to put their children on guilt trips. Having observed Hap's mother, she knew more about guilt trips than she wanted to. But his words stung. She was probably more concerned about the children than anybody else. She knew couples who'd stayed together "for the sake of the children" and watched them struggle through the misery, watched their children watching them. This was best, even for the children. She could be a better mother happy she'd told herself over and over. That was the best, the most soothing thought to stay with.

Her mother was as normal as a well-serviced clock when they arrived. She hugged the children first, peeked at the baby, poked around his chin and made little goo-goo sounds, then moved through her usual motions of helping the children take their bags to their room at the end of the long hallway of the ranch-style house that still smelled like new after fifteen years. Her parents had left a home in town and built in the country to live on the family land. Her aunts and uncles, cousins, brothers, all lived in an area of a few square miles. A community of their own. A family reunion would be a strange occasion for them.

She took the baby to her old room across the hall from the children's. She'd been too nervous and distracted in the car to nurse. This was home and it was still and quiet and not going anywhere. She could rest and relax for a few moments with little Michael, named after her oldest brother. That had widened the rift with Hap's mother, though the rest of his family could care less. Mrs. Pasley had wanted the baby named after her father, Hap's grandfather, Jesse, a good Old Testament name, not to mention a good family name, she argued. Hap's mother was wrapped, bound up in family name like a caterpillar in a cocoon, a dead caterpillar at that.

Lizzie sat in the rocker beside the baby bed, which had been hers and her brothers and pulled up her blouse and brassiere. She watched as little Michael whimpered and rooted until his moving lips found her nipple and began gurgling with nourishment, the sound of peace.

Supper was on the long table in the kitchen. Hot biscuits and cornbread. Several bowls of steaming vegetables—string beans, butter beans, corn on the cob, fried okra and hominy. Country ham. Red-eye gravy. Some leftover fried chicken from lunch. Home-dilled pickles and home-made relish. She noted her mother had removed one chair and adjusted the others to cover the missing space. Kevin and Ruthie muttered along with her father who didn't rush through his usual grace—"Bless, O Lord, this house and all therein. Bless this food to the nourishment of our bodies and us to thy service." He paused a few moments, as though he'd add something new. "In Jesus name we pray. Amen."

Everything proceeded in its normal order. Her mother was seeing to that.

The children didn't go to bed gently or orderly. Teeth brushing and vitamins: forgotten. Pottying: remembered when they were back in bed up again and back to bed. Prayers: Kevin remembered and Ruthie followed him to the floor on her knees. Their father always helped put them to bed, knelt with them and said prayers. Usually, he read a Bible story from their Bible

Story Book. These were the memories that ambushed her, just when she was feeling confident and sure again. The questions the children asked with the covers under their tiny chins and their eyes on the ceiling were the invasions she'd feared the most.

"Mommy, why are you and daddy getting a divorce?" Kevin said.

She was sitting on Ruthie's bed, had expected the first onslaught, if and when it came, from her. Her curiosity was like her grandmother's, without the subtlety. Kevin reminded her of that sleepy, but solid bond between father and sons, usually aroused when daddies were absent, especially in summer. He'd lose more. Granddaddy would be there a while longer. His uncles who could help with fishing, hunting, playing ball and all of the other natural energies of boyhood. The lawyer said Hap could get them every other weekend and six weeks in the summer, some extra days around holidays. She was hoping against hope old Judge Tollison wouldn't hear the case. He made recent history when he left the house to the children and made the parents rotate in and out. She didn't want the house and didn't want the kids wanting the house or anything connected with it. She wanted a clean break from the place which, looking back on it, had been nothing but a trap. She'd been tricked into loving someone who wasn't what she'd thought he was and confined on thirty acres of idle land deader than the love she'd once had.

"Mommy, you aren't answering my question." His mouth was curled into a soft pout, but his flared pupils were the end of a double-barrel aimed through his tired and sleepy eyes.

"Sometimes two people who are married decide they're so different they can't live together anymore," she said.

"Daddy looked like he was just one person," Kevin said, the loaded look still on his face.

"Mommy, what's a family?" Ruthie said. The question offered relief, but her daughter's eyes were beginning to look like her son's.

"Well, it's a group of people who love each other very much and do things together."

"I wanna talk about my daddy," Kevin said, pushing himself up in bed.

"That's fine, Kevin. You can talk about your daddy anytime you want to." She was trying to keep her voice low and hide her panic. "He will always be your daddy."

"Mommy, are we still a family?" Ruthie said.

"Why, yes ... yes ... yes we are." Such a small word, yes, yet sometimes so hard to say. And the damage it could inflict, this slow rope she was coiling about herself.

"I wanna tell my daddy good night," Kevin blurted.

Like a meat cleaver, his comment came down hard in the middle of her patience. Try not to overreact, she told herself. They're just children. "Son, he knows we're here and—"

"Nobody asked us," Ruthie said, not whiney but in a deep adult voice.

"What? What do you mean?" she said.

"Well, if families are people who do things together, and if we're still a family, nobody asked us kids. We're family, too."

"Yeah," said Kevin. "If little Mike was bigger, it'd be three of us wanting to be asked."

Her mind spun, thought fragments swirling. Their eyes were a mixture of sleep and hurt and something else that drove straight at the heart of breath itself, something bigger than all of them. The flash of an answer came, but before she could open her mouth, Ruthie lunged.

"Mama, do you like Mr. Billy Ray?"

She felt weak and alone and scared. Her rings cut into her fingers.

"Why, no, sweetheart, except only as a friend. Why do you ask me that?" Tremor raced across her shoulders, down her arms.

"He's been there, at our house, a few times we got off the school bus, and ... well—"

"He's been there when our daddy wadn't there," Kevin said, "and we want our daddy here."

Pray. A prayer. She was cornered with nowhere else to turn but God. She knelt in the floor between their beds and reached for their hands. "Ruthie. Kevin." She looked at each of them. "I wanted your daddy here, too. Why don't we just say our prayers and ask the good Lord to help us through this?"

"Hmph," Ruthie muttered, glancing at Kevin. He glanced back. A private message passed between them before they turned their faces slowly back to her, little faces no longer angry but touched, in the corners of their lips and eyes, with grief.

"Did I say something wrong?"

They looked at each other again but said nothing.

"Well, bow your heads and close your eyes."

Her mind a vacuum, voided of anything creative, the prayer she said was one memorized from her childhood, its final words, "guide me safely through the night and wake me with the morning light," a hope for each of them. Then there was nothing was left inside her.

She knew her mother had been waiting to talk. It wouldn't include her father, and rarely did when serious matters were at hand. He'd go to sleep in the recliner with the television going, on through the news. Her mother would never wake him and say it's time but climb into bed by herself; go to sleep, by herself, as if that was all she needed. Liz wondered now what, or who, they leaned on. Both good people, they moved within their own boundaries, their own worlds of habit, with little show of affection. She couldn't remember the last time she saw her father kiss her mother, even hug her. It was as though at some point in their long years together they'd mutually agreed to routine, or the fire just went out, slowly, like a fire will when it's not tended and fed. Maybe it was the routine that kept them together, routine plus God. She'd been afraid to ask why, afraid she'd discover some dark and deep hurt that needed to stay buried. She prayed again, this time that her father would stay awake tonight. She needed that protection.

Her mother sat on the couch, knitting something. She sat in the other recliner across from her father. *Hee Haw* on television was little relief. *Lawrence Welk* was next. They watched with fake interest, through the commercials, without conversation.

Finally, her mother made her move. "Well, I've got to turn in. It's been a long day. You going soon, hon?" It was a woman-to-woman's hint, ever so subtle, but clear as the dimming of distant car lights on a long lonely stretch of road.

She leaned forward in the recliner to accept the kiss her mother placed in the usual spot on her forehead.

"I'll be along after a while, mother. I just need to wind down." From what, she couldn't tell her; she was still trying to figure out for herself. Whoever's genes her children had inherited, and they weren't Hap's, probably not hers either, would be coming at her again.

Her father's recliner was cocked as far back as it would go. He lay with his head to one side, his eyes closed. The noises, clinks and tinkles from her parent's bathroom across the hall seemed louder than usual. More hints to hurry up. She felt sorry for her mother. She'd never intruded into her life and knew now her feelings were coiled knots of apprehension and curiosity. They'd just have to wait till morning to loosen their hold on her. One knot couldn't untie another.

The news came on from the station in Tupelo, the largest town in north Mississippi. It was usually about local happenings in that part of the state, the spicy stuff at first. A man arrested for the murder of his wife in Okolona. A marijuana field discovered by undercover narcotic agents near Ecru. A drug bust in a housing project in Tupelo. The silver-haired weatherman said a strong cold front was moving through the area bringing rain, possibly turning to sleet and snow by morning. Until then, she'd given little notice to the increasing gusts of wind through the wind chimes in the carport, against the shutters and storm door.

Throughout the news segments and commercials, her thoughts shifted back and forth from Hap to Billy Ray, from her children to her parents, sometimes just from herself to herself, questions more than answers, hurts more than solutions to hurts.

Her mother leaned her head in the door one last time, her face aged in the short time she'd prepared for bed. "Good night, hon. You're in my prayers," she said.

She couldn't say it, but she was glad. She needed to be in somebody's prayers, somebody who still had a connection with the Almighty. If anyone did, it was her mother. She nodded and blew her a goodnight kiss and said she'd see her in the morning, feeling guilty as she did it. But guilt was better than baring her soul to someone who might not be able handle what was there, and she'd surely bare her soul if she started talking now.

Ed McMahon was saying, "Now, Her-r-r-r-r-re's Johnny," and her father raised up and clicked the recliner forward.

"You still up, Sis?"

"Yessir. Just needed to wind down."

"Well, check the heat. Weatherman said it might get cold tonight." He had an amazing ability to sleep or nap or drowse or drift into whatever half-world he entered in his recliner and still collect whatever it was that was important to him on the television. She had to smile at that.

He leaned over and kissed her on the same spot her mother had kissed her. Eyes closed, she could tell their kisses apart. Not so much by the shape or warmth of their lips but by their pressure and duration. Her father's, firm and lengthy. Her mother's, light and brief. Both, reassuring and comforting, accepting, pledges she could lean on and go to sleep with. Tonight, of all nights, she'd need all of it.

She waited until the light went out across the hall in their bedroom before she disconnected the telephone from the wall jack above the kitchen counter. She removed her shoes and tiptoed down the hallway to her room where she reconnected the small plastic plug in the receptacle beside her night table, the same connection she'd used when she lived there, the same one when she dated Hap and couldn't see him.

The smells of the room—cedar and mothball and lemon-scented furniture wax—embraced her with her youth and memories of endless hours of talking on the telephone and listening to her clock radio, everything freshly preserved as though she were expected, at any moment, as though her mother knew. Even the sheets were neatly folded back and across their straight unwrinkled edge, her favorite dolls, arranged side-by-side, leaning against the only frilled pillows she'd ever known. Why did she ever leave that, a family and a farm and a college degree?

The light from the small lamp on her night table was enough. A shaky finger punched at the numbers on the receiver. Hap had never spent a night by himself in his entire life. The fact he'd not called was troubling. Think, Liz. Why are you doing this, calling to check on someone you wish you couldn't even remember remembering? She listened, attaching answers to the rings, each whir a question drilling her ear. To make sure the dog was fed. She'd never seen Hap use a can-opener in her life. To make sure the stove was turned off. He wouldn't know a front eye from a back eye, much less the knob that turned them on and off, or the oven either. He was the children's father. She owed him that much. She still loved him though she wasn't "in love" with him. This was the Christian thing to do. She'd worked that limp logic before. Simply because he hadn't called, which she'd expected, and because he hadn't, he was doing something else such as drinking again, which meant he was becoming more focused, or unfocused, on who was across the road from him than on her.

An alarm, separate from her body and a long way off, yet ringing as though it were coming through the receiver, stopped her. She felt she had more than just two lungs and one heart working inside of her.

Maybe she mis-dialed.

She tried again. Still nothing.

She could go back down the hallway to the den and get the telephone directory. But that might wake her parents.

She punched zero.

"Information," the operator said.

"The Bedford County Sheriff department, please."

4

Hap

His eyes finally made out the tiny pores and straight cement lines of a concrete block wall. He touched his face first and rubbed his eyes then touched the wall to make sure it, too, was real. The stench of urine and mildew and somebody else's old body odor moved his hand quickly to his nose which he grabbed and clamped to keep from gagging. He could hear a radiator hissing nearby and voices mumbling in the distance. He turned over and saw green bars surrounding him, and the realization of where he was suddenly aroused him. When he sat up, his brain slid like a huge load in an empty truck on a sharp turn. Pain slammed against his eyes. Another throbbed in his ankle. A dull nausea in his stomach and a burning throat connected him with part of the night.

Never in his life had he been in jail and never imagined he would be. That thought was about as foreign to him as divorce. Lizzie. Another piece of the night fell into place. He groaned, struggling for others, anything to help him put the memory back together. A few images floated before him—the fire, Homer, pictures, his fist shattering the gun case window. The gun?

"Hey!" he shouted. The word echoed through the cold concrete and steel like a loudspeaker throwing it back at him, for nothing else came.

"Hey!" Louder this time. "Anybody there?"

The click of footsteps. Down a long hallway, a door clanged open. The footsteps clicked with a loud evenness. Through the spaces of the bars, he made out the face coming toward him. Joel Rooker, a deputy. They'd been in high school together, Joel two years ahead of him. He was heavier and swung his weight with an exaggerated uppity air. Joel Rooker had never amounted to much in school, but he'd helped the new sheriff's campaign, and now he was somebody.

"We wondered if you was coming back into the world," Rooker said, unsmiling as he slipped a key into the cell door and swung it open like a pasture gate.

"How did I—"

"We thought you was dead when we found you." He hooked a thumb up the hallway toward the door. "Sheriff Cramden saw you first. Took one look at the shotgun and them pictures and thought sure to God you was a corpse."

"But how—"

"Then he leaned over and smelled and said you were skunk drunk. So, we brung you here.

"I still don't—"

"Your wife called us, 'bout eleven. Said she'd been trying to phone you, that ya'll had a fuss or something, which ain't none of our business, but thought maybe we'd better check on you."

"Then I—" Recalling too many movies he'd seen, he stopped himself. "Damnit, Rooker. Just read me my rights then let me make my phone call."

"Ain't no charges, Hap."

"What? You mean to tell me—"

"I said, there're ain't no charges. Gun and pictures are in the office. I'll drive you home."

The words relieved only his thoughts. As he stood in the cell doorway, the load in his brain rolling now like a runaway bowling ball, he grabbed onto a bar to ease the weight on his right foot which felt like a spike had been driven all the way into his calf.

"I think I need to see a doctor."

"For a hangover?"

Carefully, he pulled up his pants leg.

"Shit a'mighty, man! That thing's swole big as a fence post. Sheriff, git in here. What'd you tangle with?"

"Black widow."

A stocky man, broader across the shoulders and shorter than Rooker, waddled hurriedly to where they stood.

"Take a look at that, Sheriff," Rooker said. "Ain't that the most godawful bite you ever seen. Looks worse'n a bullet wound."

"Sure as shit does. You need to git that thing seen about, Pasley. We thought you was dead. Hadn't been for your wife, you might still be out there, frostbit for sure, not to mention whatever tore into your leg like that."

Frostbit. As if he needed more to confuse him. "Frostbit?"

"Yep," the sheriff said. "Snowing out there now. Didn't do nothing but sleet and ice most of the night. Roads are slick as froze snot."

Rooker's eyes were still glued to his leg.

"That sucker came on like a bear in winter," the sheriff continued. "Weatherman called it some kind of upper air dee-sturbance, somethin' like that. Never seen nothing like it."

With no window, he had to believe them. His first thoughts were of Lizzie and the children. They were safe. "Was my dog there, I mean, when you found me?"

"Laying right beside you," Rooker said. "Run off up toward the house. Lights and all must've spooked him."

"The house. Was it still there?"

Rooker removed his neon orange hunting cap and scratched the back of his head. "Hot damn, Hap. We sure 'nough got to git you to a doctor. Question is, which kind? What do you mean, was the house still there? We didn't say nothing 'bout no tornado. Sure, it was there. Lit up like a Christmas tree. We rode up and checked on it. Looked like you really tied one on, or somebody did. Porch ceiling caved in on one side. Insides looked like a burglar had a fight with the fireplace. We locked her up for you."

"I'm much obliged. Things aren't going too well right now and—"

"Like I said, ain't none of our business," Rooker said. "Just glad to be of help."

"Don't reckon one of you fellas could get me over to Doc Boswell's to see about this leg?"

"Sure 'nough," said Rooker. "Got chains on the patrol car. We can cut right through that white stuff like a hog through slop."

Sheriff Cramden nodded his approval.

"Ain't you gonna call Lizzie first?" Concern coming from Joel Rooker sounded rare. What he said next wasn't. "She knows you're here. We called her after we found you."

"Oh no!"

"Don't worry," Rooker said. "We didn't tell her you was drunk, just in a ditch. Just show her that leg."

She already knew about his leg, and that would help. For a moment he almost wished the cold had claimed him. He'd heard freezing to death was the most painless way to go. Not on the inside though. Being cold there was the worst pain of all. No doctor could relieve that.

"It'll be sore for a day or so," Dr. Boswell said after applying an ointment on the dark red sore that was now larger than a throwing washer. He was a squat, heavy set man, old enough to retire, but he never had. "Folks around here won't let me," he always said when asked then rambled on about how no doctor, young or old, would come to a place that wasn't big enough or rich enough to build him a big house with a swimming pool, buy him a Mercedes or pay for his cruises or vacations to Europe and Destin, that the government would have to pay a doctor to come to a place like Hatchie, Mississippi. His face was fat and fell in folds down to his neck. Thick, blubbery lips hid a slight speech problem when he spoke. "These spider bites are all different, some worse than others. The center there" he pointed at it, "will get real black, and the necrosis will spread some and the skin may peel away, but you won't lose anything. Had to amputate a lady's leg once though, from the knee down. Brown recluse. But you'll be okay. Put this ointment on it every few hours or so, and take these pills. They'll help some."

He thanked Doc Boswell and paid him thirty-five dollars, thanked him for coming down to his office on a Sunday morning, then walked toward the idling patrol car at the curb where Rooker sat waiting. His feet crunched in the snow, but underneath, he knew there was ice on the concrete walkway. He walked carefully, slowly.

The doctor's office was a small brick building on the eastern rim of the town, so with only a turn of his head, his eyes marked its four corners—the elevator shaft of the old cotton gin, the steeple of First Baptist Church, and the two snow-capped water towers. One silver-coated like new served the factory and the other, rust-streaked, was the town tank where a prankster several years back had painted over the last two letters to make the name read HATCH. Ice-coated power lines threaded leaning utility poles like thin glass cables holding it all together. Somewhere, through the middle of that misty, wintry acreage of homes and stores and blackened leafless trees, invisible under the snow, ran the state highway, the only way out to any place important. The colorless white world looked like a patched-up dream that would go away as soon as it came, knowing as the thought moved through him that only the white would go away and nothing else. He wished he could know another world, not even a different one. Just another small town would do.

His face stung in the brittle bitter cold. Without a coat, the rest of his body numbed quickly. The temperature had to be below freezing and by the looks of it, four or five inches of snow covered the ground, a few flakes still falling here and there, a sign the worst was probably over, for the weather anyway.

What would he do next? Where would he go? Back to an empty house with an empty kitchen and swing set and sandbox, a place that could no longer give to him, only take big chunks from him until it got to his heart, then rip it out and wring it dead. Go back to some devilment in the air that took over him? He had a married brother twenty miles north just over the Tennessee state line, two married sisters in Memphis, and another married brother in Little Rock. But they had small children, some near the age of his. He couldn't bear that, being around children that weren't his. A single cousin lived in Tupelo. But he was into drugs, possibly even selling them. He thought quickly before he reached the car and would need to tell Rooker where to take him. Nothing promising came to mind.

As he neared the car, Rooker rolled down his window a few inches and yelled through the crack. "Pasley, git your ass in here 'fore you freeze solid and I have to drag you in again."

The warmth of the patrol car was an uncertain comfort. He rubbed his hands and went through the motions of thawing, stalling for more time to think.

"What'd the doc say?" Rooker asked.

"That I'd live."

"And you paid for that?" He felt Rooker trying to humor him. Rooker was probably better at that, humoring folks than deputying. He fit in better with the whittling crowd around the courthouse.

"Yep. 'Fraid so. He said I wouldn't lose nothing. If he only knew."

"She'll come back. Probably got a cob up her rear or that PMS shit that gives 'em all an excuse for wolf-bitching." He spat a brown stream in a Mason jar he kept cradled in his lap. "Then they go back to being sunshine sweet like a dark cloud passed through 'em and ever'body else saw it but them. 'Sides, women cain't stand to see a man weak. Go rent you a good kick-ass, shit-on-'em John Wayne movie. Treat 'em like dirt, and they love you for it."

He could almost chuckle at that, wanted to believe her leaving and taking the kids had something to do with her time of the month. That would be easy. It would be easy even thinking it was just Billy Ray. But the more he tried to throw the blame on something or somebody else, the more it returned to him, like a boom-o-rang or a yo-yo. Probably a yo-yo, which was how he felt and had for all of the life he remembered. Some strange force or circumstance that had no connection to him would throw him out. Then, zip. Right back again. The times he wanted to fight it or get at it, he ended up hitting or hurting himself because nothing else made sense to hit or hurt. Except last night, and what gave him the sense, saved Billy Ray.

Liquor. So, he said the only thing next he could think to say. "I'd give up my arms and legs and rest easy in a wheelchair to the end of my living days just to have my family back, Rooker. That's all I live for."

Rooker just stared at him like it was getting too deep, even for someone tough acting as him. "Where to, Pasley?"

"Mama's. Just take me to Mama's. She lives—"

"I know. Past your place out the Black Zion road. You got it."

The car lurched forward. Silence took over. He was glad. He needed to think. Not just what to tell his mother, which he feared the most, but Lizzie when he called he,r which was the next thing he needed to do. The thought stirred old nerves where he always felt them first, somewhere deep in his stomach.

Nothing else was moving. The town lay hushed, a strange frozen landscape. Only on a Sunday would it have been like that, snow on the ground in Mississippi and nobody playing in it. His watch said almost noon. Everybody was in church. Nothing kept people from church in the Bible Belt. They'd close schools and factories and cancel D.A.R. meetings if the sky shook out even a flurry. But not church.

He'd heard people say if the factory hadn't come to town, the town would've dwindled to nothing within a few years, that it was headed that way. He thought if the churches pulled up stakes overnight and left, the town would be gone about as quickly. Not moved. Destroyed, by its own, because there'd no longer be anything or anybody to remind them of sin and guilt and hell, fear of the last being the real glue that held this place and others like it in the South together. Yessir, ever'body, 'cept derelicts and outlaws and drunks who didn't believe in hell, was in church today.

The car turned a corner, and beyond a row of small homes First Baptist came into view on his right, and he felt a sudden assault on his soul. He would've been there today with Lizzie and the kids. They would've sat together on the right side, second pew from the front, the same pew where he sat the moment something told him she was the one he'd marry. Sitting there on Sunday mornings had become a tradition for them, one he'd settled into and honored as sacred as prayer, and thought she had too. It was the one spot where all his troubles ended and any threat was a far off murmur and every tomorrow secure, especially when their hands reached for each other behind the kids and clasped and held during the choir's singing of the final benediction. He was a long way from that now.

As they approached the church, the front doors opened, and people emptied into the snow they had trampled getting there. A handful of children scampered ahead, fanning into the smooth untouched lawn where they tumbled and rolled like wild monkeys. He crouched low in the seat, just enough to see above the dash and bottom of the window. His eyes scanned for Lizzie and the kids as the scene moved toward him. They would be there.

Soon he saw them, she at the door shaking Brother Hammingtree's hand, Ruthie and Kevin streaking after the other children into the large churchyard. He watched his children for a moment, how happy they seemed, how normal, how not daddy-less. He wondered if they even missed him, knew he was alive. Then he glanced back at the doorway where she stood, still talking to Brother Hammingtree. He strained hard to see her face which was wrapped in a red muffler, one he'd given her last Christmas. The scene was sliding past him, and he craned his neck around in an effort to hold it as long as possible, fighting the pain in his head which moved every time he moved. By the way her head was bobbing, he could tell she was still the one talking. Brother Hammingtree took her hand and patted it and said something to her, then a cluster of trees cut them off. He twisted and caught a last glimpse of her through the wire mesh that separated the front and back seats of the patrol car. She was on the top step calling and waving. He needed it to be for him as he saw the children high-stepping through the snow toward her.

He turned around. Now his pastor knew. Others were standing near. Surely they'd know, too. If she was just thinking it over, she wouldn't be telling anybody. She wasn't the kind to talk just for the sake of talking. If she was telling people, then it was really over. With Rooker in the car beside him, he had nowhere for his tears to go. Rooker was the dam that kept them backed up to his eyeballs, bursting to get out, and he was stuck with him for another fifteen miles.

They passed First Methodist and the small Presbyterian Church and entered Main Street when Rooker said he could sit up now, the coast was clear. He scooted up slowly and tried to distract himself by looking in the store windows, some already decorated for Christmas. A stuffed Santa Claus in the Western Auto store rode a three-wheeler. Next door in Sears, a large red ribbon and bow packaged a washer and dryer. The sign on top said THIS CHRISTMAS MAKE HER A QUEEN. He bit his lip to keep his crying locked down.

They crossed the railroad tracks and turned south onto the state highway, passing the blinking portable arrow signs at Johnny's One Stop and Reba's Bar-B-Q and R J's Pit Stop before heading into a bright white wonderland that stretched flat from both sides of the road into distant hills where trees were tangled webs of scratches on the gray horizon. Cedars flared like dark green flames along fence rows. Above them, strings of black birds knotted along sagging power lines. Random patches of broomgrass took on a brighter orange color in the snow. Punctuating the scene were sounds of static from the police band radio, wind rushing along the windows, the rattling of tire chains through the snow and Rooker spitting every now and then into his Mason jar. For the first time, he noticed the clutter around him. Ticket pads and pens and clipboards scattered across the dash. Empty Styrofoam cups and chewing gum wrappers on the floor. A pair of handcuffs and a holstered pistol on the seat beside him. It was not a place he needed to be but one he must endure for the eternity it took to get to his Mama's, and they had to pass his house on the way. He braced himself for that.

Rooker stared straight ahead over the steering wheel for a few miles before breaking the silence. "How's the pencil farming going?"

He hadn't heard that phrase in a while, and the words cut him. If Rooker hadn't looked so innocent, he'd have told him to stop the car and let him out. Maybe it was Rooker's way of trying to help him out. Talking.

"If you mean my land being in the soil bank, it's fair-to-middling. Brings a check. Pays a bill or two. Why?"

"Just wondered. Never thought I'd live to see the day Big Brother'd pay a man not to plant his own crops." He spat again.

"Seemed the thing to do at the time. Still does. Not much in farming anymore, not 'round here anyways. Big farm corporations up north and out west running the show. They're the only ones making money these days with it. Politicians ain't never done nothing for the little farmer, 'cept make him bunches of promises when they needed his vote. Soil bank may be the only decent thing government ever did for us farmers, least ways down here in flat broke Mis'sippi."

"And you like it better all closed up in that fact'ry, doing the same thing all day, slaving for somebody else? That'd drive me plum nuts. If it was me, which it ain't you understand, I'd feel like I done went and sold my soul. 'Member that song Tennessee Ernie Ford sang once, 'Sold my soul to the company store,' something like that, yessir, makes me think of that."

He glanced over at Rooker, at his jaw working the tobacco as though that was where all his thinking was taking place. Rooker looked all smug in his deputy uniform sunk in behind the wheel of a sheriff's patrol car, like all that plus a badge and gun elevated him to position of teacher of knowledge and qualified him to spit out more than Days Work tobacco juice. What he was saying hadn't worked itself up to his brain yet for him to realize that sitting around a jailhouse all day watching soap operas and riding around in the same car owned by the county, traveling the same roads, wasn't exactly the opposite of boredom, not to mention his job was owned by the county and the bootleggers and the next election and him talking about selling his soul. But in open countryside in below freezing weather and him with no coat and no money he wasn't going to get into it with the man driving the car, not much anyway.

"You really know how to hurt a guy, Rooker. You're 'bout to piss me off."

"No harm meant, Pasley. Just trying to help. If it was me, which like I said it ain't—"

"Damn right it ain't you, and all's I need you to do right now is guide this here bubble top to my Mama's."

"Just hold your horses a minute, Pasley, and lemme finish. Now if I had that place of yours right yonder," he pointed off to the left.

"Let up, Rooker."

Across the glare of land, he saw the house atop the lonely hill, looking lonelier in the trackless snow. The porch tilted downward on one side like something crippled and abandoned, home now for only a dog that lay dug in under its old flooring. That was the next thing he'd planned to replace so when the real estate people walked folks over it, they could say, "And it's got a new floor, too." He blinked. For a moment, he saw children squealing in a homemade sled, careening down the hill, parents waving and shouting from the porch. His mind worked against his eyes then against itself, against a memory not yet a day old that said it was so, then gave in. Nobody lived there now. If only she could've waited. In another month or two, he would have walked into the kitchen and laid the papers on the table, and she would have smiled big and kissed him and pulled him into the bedroom and shut the door with supper still bubbling on the stove and rewarded him. If only. He needed that thought now, let it play over and over until—

"Pasley, dammit, let me finish. If that was my place, I'd rent me a bulldozer, do a little earth work, lay a few pipes from the Hatchie River yonder, and raise catfish. Folks up north scarfing up catfish like it was the last poontang on earth. You could sit on that porch and watch your money break the top of the water each eve'nin' and flip your finger at that damned fact'ry that laid all you boys off, even flip it at the weather, too. Hell, catfish live on bad weather and this place is—"

"Turn in!"

"What? In your drive? Thought you was going to your mama's."

"Changed my mind. Just turn in."

"Now wait a minute, Pasley. I didn't mean to get you all riled up. Let's just go on to your mama's, what a ya say?"

"Nope. I need to check on Homer and see he's fed." That was part true. The other part was only his to know.

"Shit, Pasley, if you don't beat all. I can barely see the turn-in much less that half-assed road up to your house. The thing's under at least a half-foot of snow. This ain't no four-wheel Jeep."

"Fine. Just let me out here. I'll walk."

"Suit yourself. Guess those boots can take you there without your feet breaking off. You're actin' more like you been snake-bit than spider-bit."

He got out and felt the wet cold snap in around his ankles first before the frigid seepage around his soles hit the sides of his feet.

"Much obliged, Rooker, for everthing. I'll vote for ya'll next time 'round. Wouldn't want you to have to go looking for a job." He couldn't resist the jab and watched Rooker's face screw up before he spat a mouthful into the jar.

"Shit, Pasley. That's all I gotta say. I hope you get yours together. Here're your keys." He pulled a ring of three keys from his pocket, one to the house and the others to his pickup. "They was on the countertop in the kitchen. We used 'em to lock up last night. Don't forget your gun and pictures in the back seat."

"Much obliged again."

He opened the back door and retrieved the gun and pictures. The second he shut the door, Rooker revved the motor, and the car crunched off.

Homer came leaping toward him, kicking snow in the air with his hind legs. His breath and tongue felt warm on Hap's hands as he reached over to receive him, rubbing the dog's face in his hands. Off to the side, like an unfinished snowman, was a round lump in the snow. The kids' clothes. He remembered. He shook the snow from the bundle and lifted it onto the porch. Homer nuzzled around his legs, staying close. The dog had to be hungry. He could use a bite himself.

The screen door barely hung from its hinges. It would only be good for fire kindling. He'd have to replace it. The first positive thought of the day stopped him, surprised him. A painful thought too. Fix it for who.

He jiggled the key and it finally turned the lock. The ruined silence and smoky light into which he stepped closed in quickly around him, as though it were alive and had been waiting. The cold kept him moving. Glass crunched under his feet as he walked quickly to replace the shotgun in the shattered case, breaking the barrel first to check the shells. Rooker must have removed them, thinking he'd meant to use them on himself. Liquor and a spider bite saved Billy Ray and kept Hap from picking cotton at the state penitentiary in Parchman for the rest of his life. He moved the furnace dial, and the heat clicked on. He wouldn't be there long, but any relief from the cold was heart welcomed.

When he laid the pictures on the coffee table, face up where they looked at him, all of the feelings loaded up in his head broke loose again.

He felt a release when he finished crying, but little comfort. If he could only be a sieve and let the pain flow through him. Instead, it just kept stopping up. The things he needed, usually kept stored up, were gone, used up, wasted. Prayers. Favorite Bible verses. Even the word God. Whoever said hell was fire and brimstone hadn't been where he was. You could feel fire and brimstone. They'd at least make you mad. Hell was not having anything left inside of you to fall back on.

He glanced down at Homer lying at his feet, the large brown eyes glimmering up at him. They looked as sad as his felt, and as hungry.

He walked into the kitchen, the world that was hers, with her smells and her sense of order. He felt like an intruder as he searched for and finally found a can of Alpo on the floor of the pantry. He marveled at the tiered shelving of detergents, canned foods, staples, glass jars, folded grocery sacks, all neatly arranged and in place, as she always kept them. The can opener was not as easy to find. It was in the last drawer he tried, lying under an assortment of strange-looking gadgets, each of which surely had a use for something. Had she been there, she'd have told him to get out and let her tend to matters. He tried several different angles before the opener finally clipped into place on top of the can. He turned the handle and the can turned and the top began to come open. He shook the can over an aluminum pie pan he found under the sink. In one sucking sound, a huge single gob of Alpo popped out and fell into the pan. Homer attacked the gooey clump like it was a shot coon fallen from a tree.

The phone call to Lizzie and the kids was next. They would have had time by now to drive to her parents from church. Ask to speak to the kids first he'd decided. That wouldn't be denied. Even if Lizzie didn't want to talk to him, she'd never keep him from the children. She was good for her word about most things. Marriage vows she was treating like they belonged in a separate compartment of her conscience. He'd been the opposite. He'd told her little lies every now and then, usually about money and finances and his drinking, but had never thought of leaving her. Nor had he gone to bed with another woman, though he came close once. At the plant, temptation existed every day, bringing some truth to his father's prediction about factories being the ruination of Southern life and morals. "Mark my word," he said once, "Them fact'ries ain't nothing but workshops of the devil, taking good men and women from the land and throwin' 'em all together sweatin' under one roof. Mark my word, that shirt fact'ry'll become a curse." Hap worked side by side with women all day long. They flirted with him.

One outright propositioned him, told him she'd do things to him that'd make him forget his wife, or any other woman, forever. Ramona Waycaster. She was tall with gorgeous blond hair, long legs that fit her blue jeans like a tight glove, and a face with eyes that would've passed for Barbara Mandrell. All the other guys dreamed about "rocking Ramona" and she came on to him like a mink in heat. He punched in the numbers on the wall phone in the kitchen. After several rings, Lizzie's father answered.

"Mr. Turpin, this is Hap. May I speak to the kids."

"Just a minute," his voice clipped, emotionless.

Ruthie spoke into the phone first, quick hello, I love you, goodbye. Though hurried, her voice was gift enough. He imagined who was hovering over her. She'd always been a quiet child, closer to her mother. Mothers and daughters. That was normal he told himself in a moment he needed reassurance.

Kevin came on. "I love you, Daddy. I miss you," the words a shock of joy.

"I love you and miss you, too. You be a good boy for your mama. You hear?"

But he didn't. Another ear received them.

"I'll tell him for you. He's playing with his granddaddy." Lizzie's voice had a strained matter-of-factness about it, but not as cool as he'd expected. It caught him off guard. He'd given no thought to what he'd say to her. His heart was racing, and he could feel the receiver shaking in his hand.

"I miss you."

She waited a long time before answering. "I miss you too, Hap. I'd be lying if I said I didn't. But I think this is best. What happened to you last night? I was worried sick. Mr. Rooker said they found you in a ditch but that you were all right."

"I ... ah ... the spider bite. Me and Homer walked down to the road, and I must've passed out. Don't know what happened. Doc Boswell treated it this morning. Said I'd be okay. Gave me some ointment to put on it and pills to take."

"Thank God. I thought you might've gotten drunk and pulled something crazy, like you used to do."

"I'll be okay." He took a deep breath. "If you can't get me for the next day or so, don't worry. There're some things I need to do."

"What do you mean? What things?"

Her voice was nervous. He pressed, throwing the dice in the oldest adult game of all time. "I can't say now. Just some things. Tell the kids I'll call."

The silence tested him. He waited. The ball was in her court.

Finally, she returned it. "I don't know what you're up to, Hap Pasley, but I hope to heaven's name it's not something foolish."

He didn't know where the feeling came from or why it was there. Maybe hurt had become such a habit that any new feeling stood out. This one was satisfaction, maybe even victory. Not one over her so much, hearing her squirm, left in the dark for a change. But over himself, not feeling the yo-yo come back. He'd tuck this moment away and remember it. He said goodbye, not even adding "I love you," knowing he'd second guess himself for that the next hundred miles. His next stop wouldn't be as easy.

5

Liz

"Lend me a hand, hon, with them vegetables," her mother said to her.

Emmy Lou and Rachael, her sisters-in-law, had been practically pushed out of the kitchen and out the back door to supervise the children playing in the snow. Her mother usually ran them all out. "One woman in the kitchen's enough," she'd say. But she was about to bust to know what was going on, and why.

Keeping her back to her mother, Liz stood at the counter filling serving bowls. Her father and two brothers would be hollering if their Sunday lunch wasn't ready soon. She observed them in the adjacent den, sprawled out in their favorite spots beneath pictures of flying ducks and pointing birddogs, watching the Cowboys play somebody on the TV console that today she was glad was turned up too loud. Above it hung a large Wal-Mart picture of Jesus, the one where the eyes follow you. He'd be busy today, she thought, then looked away from his stare.

If he hadn't gotten the couch first, Hap would have been on the floor with a pillow from one of the bedrooms doubled under his head. That was the only time he looked and acted like them, or they like him, she wasn't sure which. Four grown men who waited like kings each Sunday to be fed hand and foot (every meal, for that matter), who'd starve before they'd go to the trouble to get up and open a refrigerator door much less boil water.

Fact was, they probably didn't know how to do either. Hap usually said very little, which helped him fit into their world. He didn't know much about football or farming and hunting. But she didn't need to be thinking about him and busied herself putting food on the table.

Her mother was taking a pan of biscuits from the oven, fussing under her breath about their being too brown. She was a tall, stout-looking woman, slightly stooped. She moved much slower than she used to, her effort strained. Her once tapered ankles were swollen to knee-thickness and her feet looked compressed into granny shoes she'd long since quit lacing. Knotted hands bore, too, the evidence of years of rheumatoid arthritis she denied daily was bothersome or painful. "It's just that ole arthritis acting up again," she'd say, passing it off with a flip of her hand.

"Mama, you've got to take it easy on yourself. Why don't you rest and let me finish getting lunch ready."

"Naw, now. Ain't much left to do," she said, shaking the biscuits onto a plate. She picked at them with her fingertips and flipped them over quickly, one by one. "Kids seemed glad to talk to their daddy."

Her mother was not one to outright stick her nose into anybody's business, particularly her own children. She'd just make little comments, the kind that pry you open, not for her, but for you to have a look.

"Yessum." She thought again how she was going to handle leaving a man that wasn't a drunk, hadn't beat her or run around on her (that she knew of), or abandoned her. Facing a judge would be easier.

"That's good. Them kids love their daddy."

She walked to the sink and turned on the faucet, as if the blaring television and men-talk in the den was not enough to drown out talk twenty feet away. "Now, Mama, I know what you're thinking. But this isn't the time or place to talk about it."

"That's fine. Now don't fill them butter beans too full. You know how John gets to 'em first and sloshes 'em. Just washed and ironed that tablecloth."

"I heard that, Mama," John shouted. "If you wouldn't cook 'em so good, they wouldn't get spilt."

"See," she whispered. "Just heard his name or he wouldn't have heard nothing."

Her mother nodded. "Just heard his name or he wouldn't have heard nothing."

"Well, he heard. We can talk after dinner."

The oven timer buzzed. Her mother opened the door and poked at the roast with a fork. "That roast ain't done yet, like a lot of things in life, I'm sure. Lizzie, hon, butter them biscuits 'fore they get cold."

She might as well have been sticking the fork into her. Just be quiet, she thought. If you say anything, it'll just open you up a little more. She's probably not going to stop. This is her kitchen, not to mention, her house, and her daddy's land, though she'd never remind you of that, like Hap's mother would him.

"It ain't that the grass is greener on the other side, mind you," her mother continued, looking at the tomatoes she was slicing, like she was talking to them.

"What?"

"I said, it ain't that the grass is greener on the other side. 'Cause it usually is."

"I don't know what you're talking about, Mama."

"It's the weeds folks don't ponder. Just as many of them on one side as the other, sometimes more. On the other side that is."

"Mama, I wish you'd just talk plain English," wishing she'd kept her mouth shut instead of setting herself up again.

"Folks that get divorces're just swapping one set of troubles for another."

"Who said anything about divorce?" Betrayed. Her own children. Now her own mother. Not just reading her the riot act like they did, but bringing it down on her like a jackhammer.

"Nobody did. But you didn't come here with all them suit cases just for an overnight stay."

"You women folks sound like you're getting too serious in there," shouted Frank. She'd always been close to her brothers. The tone in Frank's voice was of old times, when one or both of them would take up for her.

"You just mind your own business, Frank Earl," her mother shouted back, but only because of the television volume. She rarely ever raised her voice. When she did, it came deep and low, from the back of her throat.

"Mama, I don't want the whole world in on my problems right now. If you could just wait a little while."

She felt guilty that she'd told the preacher before telling her mother. She'd never held anything from her. If she told her what was really locked inside, she'd see the anger, feel it curl the edges of her soul like a piece of paper thrown in a fire before it flames away into blackness. "Hap and I just don't see eye to eye on things."

Silence. The kind that pushes on you, that you think you can touch and push back but don't know how.

"Put them biscuits on the table for me," her mother said flatly. "That roast ought to be ready by now." She was facing the oven, looking through the clouded window. If the roast wasn't done, her eyes would finish it. Her voice was low, somewhere around her neck. "I can get the rest of it. You check on the baby and call ever'body outside."

This was lonely. Not the long hours at home before the baby came, when Hap was at work and the kids in school. Time when she was stuck on that hill with only the television and the telephone which brought her mother instantly, every day. Not the wall she looked at when Hap made love and turned over to enter his other lover, sleep. Lonely was the distance she saw between Hap and his mother, an emptiness she knew, just knew, would never come between her and her mother. Lonely was not knowing where else to turn, including God, as though God and mother were somehow all tangled up together so when she talked to one it was as if she were talking to both. She turned and hurried down the hall.

The baby was fighting the quilted blanket like it was some terrible monster dragged up from sleep, a blanket that in a matter of months he wouldn't let go, that would take him into that same dark world and return him, safe as a bank. She gathered him into her arms. She needed to feel his heart beating against hers, needed to feel the peace again. "I'm going to nurse the baby. Tell John or Frank to call the others," she shouted, hoping the hurt was heard. To make sure, she closed the door hard. The tears came fast and ran quickly.

Soon the house was filled with the sounds of people who were happy and hungry, as hungry as the little mouth sucking on her breast. She no longer felt the soreness there, as though it had been worn down by use. Looking at the tiny life in her arms, drawing his strength from her, she wondered who was nursing whom. Facing her on the dresser were the smiling faces of a family photo taken just months ago. "This is crazy. I must be crazy," she thought. She leaned her head against the back of the rocker, closed her eyes and tried to force other thoughts, like she had forced her smile when the photographer said, "Now, everybody say, 'Happeeeeee.'" Her eyes were still shut when she heard steps coming down the hall. The measured, toiling pace of her mother. "Go ahead and tell her," she told herself. "Tell her you don't care if you're the only one in the family for generations to get a divorce that you'd rather die than stay in a marriage that died years ago that you've found somebody else. Then tell her it's all their fault, her's and her father's, the family's and the generations' that went before them."

The door opened slowly. Her mother's eyes were hard and sad, eyes that had traveled far into the future and returned with urgent news of an awful vision. Then they softened, as though memory's speed took over and raced her to another end of time and another baby and mother, rocking in the same chair. The woman who had nursed this daughter and two sons stood in the doorway, her tortured, arthritic hands gripping the knob. A faint light flowed around her giving the appearance of a crucifix balancing itself in a moment of revelation. Then she eased down onto the floor, placed her hands on her knees, and with a face as receptive as a nun's in prayer looked up at her and said, "I'm sorry, Elizabeth."

Elizabeth. She hadn't heard that in an eternity. She placed her hand on the rough, knobby surface of her mother's and felt there what swam in the eyes that searched hers, strength and healing. Her mother was true to form. She never let distance hang long in the air, even with ladies in her church she didn't like, or the ones not in her church. If heavenly grace ever needed a body to roam the earth in after the Ascension, she gladly opened the doors of her heart, before it even knocked. That was a grace Lizzie couldn't lie to, or tell the truth to either, not this truth.

"Mama, I'm sorry, too. I've neglected you, but I felt we needed the right time, and it just hasn't been there."

"There's never a right time for pain, hon. It's just there and you deal with it, on its terms, not yours."

"Yessum." Her mother knew, like she knew everything else about Lizzie without her having to speak it. The details, no. But she knew. "But I don't know what to say."

"You don't have to say anything. I was wrong trying to push it, like trying to birth something that ain't ready to be born, like it was mine. And it ain't mine, it's yours. Whatever it is, it's yours. You're the only one can deal with it."

Their hands were still touching, and Lizzie felt something being given back to her, something frightening. She wanted to send it back and say, "Here, you take it, carry it for me." That was the thought that squeezed her mother's hand.

"No, hon. You can handle it," as though blood and pulse and cells themselves carried messages that said what the brain and mouth working together could never say. "Dinner is ready. You come on when you're ready," then she arose and left.

She looked again at the picture on the dresser. The only face not smiling was little Michael's. He was asleep.

6

Hap

The truck tires rattled over the gateless cattle guard as he entered the narrow drive that tunneled through a thicket of woods that wasn't there when he was a child. Low hanging ice-laced branches spread above him, a roofed net of thin crystal tubing sparkling in splashes of gaining sunlight that broke through from time to time. At the other end of the passage, he guessed at the roadbed which he knew veered to the right and angled up a slope into the yard of the house.

The house was built by his great-grandfather after the War Between the States. As it had since his father's death twelve years ago, the two-storied frame structure looked unlived-in, deserted. Except for the weathered siding and columns across the porch and two white urns at the foot of the steps that looked dirty gray against the whiter white, the snow blotted the age of the place and gave it a neat and tidy appearance. From a round tin flue that jutted at an odd angle from the rear of the house, a trace of smoke hinted of life.

His mother lived in three rooms at the back of the house, another change after his father's passing. It was the only space she needed to "await my Maker's calling," she argued over the disapproval of everyone.

"You'll just get lonely back there, Mama," they told her.

"At my age, living and dying got one thing in common. They don't require much room," she came back. "All's I have to face in these rooms is myself and my things."

He'd never understood that, until now.

She never locked the door, or anything else for that matter. She said anything you couldn't take with you to glory wasn't worth the worry of protecting, and if anybody wanted her life a latch wouldn't stop them. So all he had to do was push on the door which squeaked open.

He entered slowly, giving time for the damp gloom of the cold living room, what was left of its memory, to accept him, as though something lurking there might not. The air was stale and musty, but the smells of childhood and growing up were somehow still alive and reached him. This had been a place of fires and fun, of laughter, warmth, of family. Now it seemed a sealed tomb, not so much to keep something from entering as from leaving, everything in its place, just as it was the day of the funeral.

Bright light winked along the edges of the drawn shades that breathed slightly in the new air. Through tattered lace around the windows and threads of gray cobwebs, a softer yellow light cast a world of ragged shadows on the sheet-draped sofa and cushioned chairs where powdery dust lay like dead frost.

Heels down first, he crossed the rough oak floor that had shifted with the house and time. An archway led to the dining room where a long table was covered with a yellowed table cloth and set with blue china and fruit-design jelly glasses and unpolished silver pieces. Everything was neatly arranged and prepared for Sunday dinner, for a family that came now only on Thanksgiving and Christmas and Easter, and then only out of a sense of duty those holidays demanded. He would have been at Lizzy's house today, as he was every Sunday for lunch. There was family there. Men in the den laid back watching the ballgame. Women in the kitchen fussing over helping, Lizzie's mama winning, running them out. Children laughing in the back playroom, some running through the long hall, laughing, giggling, happy. Her father could die, and that would never change. Maybe that was why he needed to go, yet resented going every Sunday. Too much there reminded him of what he didn't have, and wouldn't, until his children grew up and had children of their own. He'd lived for that.

Beyond the dining room was the kitchen, its light leaking around the seam of the swinging door. Across that distance he had to decide what to tell her. He felt the same dread he'd known as a child when he'd done something wrong, or something had gone wrong and it wasn't his fault. The time he and his brother were shelling butterbeans and their fingers were hurting and Buster said, "Let's pour the shells over the unshelled ones and dump 'em in the ditch," and he said no, but Buster did it anyway, and she poked through them with a stick then used it on him first. The time he decided to run away and left the note telling that he peed in the well, when he really didn't, and what happened when he got cold and finally came home in the middle of the night only to find the whole family helping with the buckets and it being his mother, not his father, who took the strap to him, and he couldn't sit for days. He couldn't think of the good things he'd done, couldn't remember being told how proud she was of him. She never had.

His insides loosened and shifted in opposite directions, and he prayed they'd go no farther as he moved slowly across the floor. Why did he fear her, old and shriveled and stooped, a woman who ran the world until his father's death, then withdrew to three rooms, not even venturing into town, leaving the house only to attend church on Sundays with his aunt who lived down the road? What was it within those bones, beneath that wrinkled flesh, that within less time than it took to look at her could melt his insides to jelly? The others had left, had somehow managed to unhook themselves and move, not just into the next county, but the next state. He was the only one who'd stayed. Why?

He stopped just short of the door. She probably knew he was there and had since he drove into the yard. That was her style, to wait. She never came onto the porch and greeted people when they drove up or welcomed them at the door or escorted them as they left. She was either on her bed with an ailment or in her rocker in the living room. If you wanted to greet or talk to or give anything to Minerva Pasley, you went to one of those two places, or waited at one until she returned from wherever she was at the time, which could have been picking flowers in the front yard in full view of your arrival, never once bothering to raise her head or notice your presence.

He breathed deeply. The only sounds were the snow dripping from the eaves of the roof like the ticking of a hundred clocks and a slow clinking coming from the kitchen, a spoon against a bowl perhaps.

He took a final step toward the door. It gave with ease to his push. Steaming heat rushed over him like an oven suddenly opened. The dull ache in his head flared, and for a moment, he saw spots and thought he would faint. He steadied himself against the door jamb while his eyes focused. She was sitting in a cane chair at a small oilcloth-covered table, her rope-veined arms curled around a small bowl, a hand spooning rice and neckbone to her toothless mouth as a child might, her bunned head bobbing to meet the dribble. She never looked up. He stood and watched as she continued eating, steadily, not chewing, just gumming. On a side plate was a darkish yellow swirl of molasses and butter where she dipped the spoon every other bite. Over the top of wire-rimmed spectacles slanting across her nosebone she finally looked up. "Come on in, son." She said it in her usual direct way. "There's enough for you if you want some."

He moved toward her, gave her a slight hug and kissed her moist forehead where the veins looked like fading streams of age. "Can't eat just now, Mama. I need to talk."

"Smell like left over liquor. Been tonkin' again. Thought you'd stopped that tomfoolishness. Well, go ahead. Talk. Ain't nothing 'round here stopping talking. Fact is, place could use a little." She mopped rice from her thin lips with a paper napkin and eyed him squarely. "You got problems."

"How'd you know?"

"Knew it the minute you drove up. Don't come 'round here no more, 'cepting when you need something," the edge more in her eyes than her voice. "Go on. That's what mamas are for. Look like you're froze to death. Stand over there next to the fire and warm yourself."

She nodded toward the ancient Coleman wood-stove she'd refused to give up. In the opposite corner, clay grids glowing, a gas heater was hissing tall blue flames, a Folgers coffee can filled with water on top, the only humidifier she'd ever known. He chose the stove. An orange fire glinted through the slits of its iron grate, but somehow it looked cooler.

"Mama, it's hotter'n July in here. Don't you think one fire's enough?"

"Would have another'n if I could. A fire's company. Now what's on your mind?" She pushed her small frame up from the table and chair and shuffled to the sink with her dishes.

He stalled. His eyes swept the small room. Every inch along the sweating walls was taken—milk can, stove, backdoor, pie safe, butter churn, ice box, a door leading to a bathroom (though she still used the cypress outhouse in good weather) and bedroom across a hallway where he visualized her bed, dressing table, chifforobe, and foot-pedaled Singer sewing machine. A short table with a wash basin and a rub board finished out the rest. The counters flanking the sink were cluttered with porcelain canisters and bluish-green Ball fruit jars of mixed sizes, a dough tray and a rolling pin, a splatter-blue tea kettle, and an assortment of crockery from which stemmed wooden handles of different lengths. Frayed cook books marked by recipes clipped from newspapers and magazines extended from one wall under a cabinet. To the left of the window above the sink hung a wire basket of onions, sweet potatoes and peppers. Lizzie couldn't stand to come here. Not because of his mother. They managed well enough together. But because of frustrated duty. "I can't go unless I help, and I can't help in a kitchen where nothing has a place," she'd said more than once.

"Well, go on," she said, rinsing dishes under the tap water.

"This is hard for me to tell you, Mama, but Lizzie took the kids yesterday and left."

Her back was to him, bent over the sink. She stiffened a moment then began working her elbows again. He waited, unsure she heard him above the water and clattering dishes and was about to tell her again when she turned. In the grayish glare of window light behind, her she looked older than her seventy-four years, but her eyes, magnified through the tiny round lens of her glasses, were ageless bluish blurs rushing at him.

"Why?"

He held his hands for strength. "Said she was tired of living in a place that wadn't hers and never would be, or ours. Believe she said 'hers.' Wanted 'her place.' Those were her words. Told her I was fixing to buy the Pullen place, that it'd be ours, with our name." Then he waited.

She stretched her arms along the sink to brace her back in that stance he knew meant a lecture was coming, one that dare not be interrupted.

"That's foolishness. Cain't name a place that was named a hun'erd years before you. Look at the Warriners. Bought the Ratliff place and cleared off what was left of what burned to the ground and put a trailer on it. Always'll be the Ratliff place, 'til enough folks die off not to remember Ratliff no more. And the Worshams. Built that mansion on land owned once by the Beauchamps and before them the Waldrops, and it'll forever be the Waldrop place. No sirree. Cain't name a land haunted by ghosts. Naming land that cain't be named ain't what caused her to leave. Got to be more to it than that."

He'd been thinking while she was talking. "Said she was tired of being married to a factory man and wanted a farmer." That was as close as he wanted to come to mentioning Billy Ray. His mother liked him. After his wife's death, she talked about him, how strong he was and steady. Even then he'd feel her sending him a message—*Now, Hap, why don't you be like Billy Ray there and work for yourself like all the rest of us have done.* Or she'd point out how Billy Ray was a tee-totaler. "You'd never find the likes of him in one of those honky-tonks." She could work guilt on him like a spell, like she was doing now with her eyes, whipping him with the stare he feared more than the flames of hell itself.

"Hmph," she grunted. "That ain't all."

Sweat trickled under his armpits. He could feel it beading on his face. A tremor he knew had no connection to a spider bite or a hangover began in his stomach and ran the length of his arms and legs. "No'm."

"Well!"

The word came at him hard, like he remembered in other times before the switching or the strapping. Only this time her arms weren't folded and she wasn't tapping her foot. To anyone else, she might have been Saint Peter astride the pearly gates asking for an accountability of his sins. But to him, she was God holding up the pillars of the temple of family name, bearing down with the face of judgment, drawing all his guilt to one point as though his confession of faith a year ago never happened, his old sins as unforgiven as ever. She'd say it was marriage, something to her more sacred than the Ten Commandments or the Golden Rule or the Sermon on the Mount put together, never to be violated or profaned in the slightest, but he knew it had everything to do with keeping the family name pure and undefiled and good, and all that coming from the woman who said you couldn't name something that had already been named a hundred years before, like family name was some rarified stream of gold. She would've made a good Jew, he thought. All of them would have. If the Bible had left off all the begats, maybe it would've all been really different, like Jesus meant it to be.

He fought the pressure to cower and defend himself with pathetic excuses that memory reminded him had never worked, only made her madder. He'd gotten drunk, he told himself, and was already paying for that. He'd not beaten his wife or betrayed her or abandoned her. He was just a prodigal who was supposed to be able to come home. By God, he was innocent and would hold to that thread until she melted in the very heat she created herself. The one thing he was guilty of was wanting to kill the son of a bitch who was taking his wife and kids away from him. That was what this was all about.

"Another man."

"Heaven's sakes alive. Surely not," saying it with the same angry amazement she probably thought or said when the doctor told her she was pregnant with him at forty-five, middle-age accident, surprise, and the rest of her children beyond college age, certainly beyond the house on the hill loaned to them to get their start, and all of them way beyond that now and her and his father too old or too exhausted in years to show him how to farm, only how to ride the mule or sit on the plow or harrow, so he was still stuck on that hill, and had been for ten years. "Heaven's sakes alive. Surely not." As though, *You done something, boy* when all he did was the only thing he knew to do, had been untrained to do, which was get a job at the new factory in town which his father cursed as though it were the anti-Christ when he should've been cursing the erection and the sperm that began him and brought him into the world.

"I don't want nothing to eat," he said. "You got nothing that'll fill me up."

He left through the backdoor. He stood on the back porch, allowing the shock of cold to work its healing, cool him from the hell he'd just left. Beyond the porch, some thirty yards, was the barn, and beside it, the long shed. Under it rested a late-model John Deere, its drive shaft as straight as the day it was bought new and around it a rusting graveyard of tongued and spidery iron-wheeled equipment—disc harrow, top harrow, middle buster, stalk cutter, plow scraper, turning plow, slip, hay rake. He knew their names. But that was all he knew.

To the east of the barn and shed, the ground sloped evenly toward a line of woods. Near the northern edge, he could see the wrought-iron fence that enclosed the family cemetery plot. The cracked marble slabs looked like tiny black tabs rising from the snow. As though carried by a breeze that blew from there, words his father had spoken on a hot, bright summer day reached him. "When machines take over from mules, son, farming for folks like us'll die. The mule may be the poorest engine ever built, and for every hour he works eats ten pounds of food, but he'll do what you tell him, and he won't break down, and he won't cause you to mortgage your land just so's you can keep up with the Jones's. Don't never mortgage or sell your land, son." From the back of the mule that pulled the plow his father guided, Hap asked why. "'Cause I talked to the Lord last night and he said he wadn't makin' no more."

The clouded sun was just above the porch gable. He thought of going back inside. But there was nothing there for him, nothing but one more rejection. He knew of a place he could go, had heard the men at the factory talk about it, where he could be nameless and lose himself, and his pain. The money he took from the nest egg he'd kept hidden in a metal box near the spot where he'd unearthed the bottle the night before would buy him that. If he left now, with the roads slick and covered with snow, he'd be there before sunset and wouldn't have to worry about sunrise.

7

Liz

The house was quiet. Her brothers and their wives and children had gone. After a late afternoon snack and exhausted from a day of rollicking in the snow, Kevin and Ruthie had fallen asleep in the den—one on the couch, one on the rug. She'd lifted and taken each to their bedroom, carefully slipped off their clothes, and tucked them under the quilts their grandmother had made for them before their supper or baths or the reading of their Bible story and the prayer she said anyway over the low murmurs of their breathing. Little Michael was asleep, too, lulled there by the movement of the rocker and the sweetness from her breast, where she felt his mouth still securely attached. By the snorts from the den, she knew her father had dozed off in his recliner. Her mother would be sitting on the couch knitting, her eyes on the slow and steady movement of her crippled hands. The television was off. Perhaps this was their interpretation of romance, the closest they probably came to it now.

On the next downward motion of the rocker, she stopped. The dresser mirror reflected a rust-colored sky from the window behind her, framing the family portrait, faces that seemed to belong to the dying light. Sunday dusk. Sunset on any other day of the week brought peace, connected her with herself and the Lord. She'd never understood why it was different on His day, why that light always seemed to carry sadness, even when she was happy, the happiness fighting to stay happy. Maybe it was because another week was over and the week ahead wouldn't be any different, that life was supposed to be more but instead would go on and on in the same sameness. And the Lord she'd worshipped and prayed to that morning, who was supposed to hear her and change it all for the better, was riding His sun instead of guiding it, as though He'd made it just for Himself, as though that was what each of us had to do, reach for whatever dreamy light we could and hold on as far as it would take us. She pushed her feet quickly on the floor and rocked again, faster.

Tomorrow. Tomorrow Hap would receive the papers from the sheriff's department. She wondered how he'd take it and felt sorry for him, that he'd have to face his pain alone. Tomorrow she'd have to look for a job in a town of three thousand and face a jillion questions. Her brothers had already told her how the job hunt would go. She could check with the store owners for a clerk's position just to be told business was down because of the factory lay off. Then she could go out to the factory and fill out the application and maybe get hired because most of the jobs were held by men and she was a woman and the Office of Equal Employment Opportunity was breathing down the necks of the fat cats up north who ran the factory, and they might face a sex discrimination suit if they turned her down. All of that was a "maybe." Her mother had the better idea. Drive to the junior college in Booneville and enroll in nursing school and have a degree in two years. She'd probably qualify for a low-interest loan or grant-in-aid. Betty Sue Brubaker got one of each when she got divorced, and Betty Sue wasn't very bright and only had a G.E.D. What none of them knew, and couldn't know, was that tomorrow wouldn't last long, that she only had to go through the motions of looking for a job, that her future was already secure on one hundred acres of land owned by one Billy Ray Rather who was there now waiting for her phone call.

The baby's mouth popped softly as she uncoupled him from her breast. She laid him in his bed, covered him, and tiptoed down the hall to the den. The longer she put off lying to her mother, the harder it became. She needed to just walk in and make it snappy, like it was something she did every Sunday evening, before her mother could ask questions and parade a list of reasons why a lady shouldn't be out driving at night by herself, much less in ice and snow.

"Looks like we're the only two humans around here still awake to the world," her mother said without looking up from her knitting. The wheezes from her father's open mouth agreed.

"If you mean by awake, our eyes being open," she said. She tried a smile. "Mother, I need to borrow the car."

"Borrow the car? What for heaven's sakes for? Only thing open on Sunday 'round here is Johnny's, and you certainly don't need to be going *there* by yourself." The look on her face was ironic—her eyes, raised behind her glasses, steady beads of suspicion.

"I need to check on the house and get a package of Pampers I forgot." Then she remembered. She'd packed the last of the Pampers. Quickly, she clutched the keys from the kitchen counter and grabbed her coat and purse from the hat tree beside the door.

Then the inevitable: "Hon, the house can wait, and we can get Huggies tomorrow at Jitney Jungle. A lady's got no business out at night by herself, especially in this weather. At least wake your dad and let him go with you."

"Shhhhh, Mother. Let him sleep. I'm a big girl. It may take a while. I promise to drive slow and take my time. There's no telling what shape Hap left the house in."

"Left? He's not there?"

"He said he was going to his mother's." She felt the weakness of the lie dribble out on the last syllables, as she did with any lie she told her mother.

"Well, go ahead, wake your dad. Eulice!"

Her father jumped and grunted, flipped his head to the other side, and slipped back into his dream world.

"I couldn't wake a face looking that peaceful. Don't worry. And don't wait up."

"Wait up?" Her arms collapsed on her knitting. "I declare. It don't take that—"

"Mother-r-r-r. I'll call if I need help." She leaned over and kissed her. "Now don't you worry yourself for nothing."

But worry, like a brittle mask, covered her mother's face. "You're still in your Sunday clothes," she said.

She pretended she didn't hear and closed the door quietly as she left.

Her face felt the cold first before the chill snapped in around her feet. She fumbled in the dark for the right key then remembered her father's old car was a gear shift and not automatic like Hap's truck, which was the only vehicle she'd driven in over ten years. Ancient memories from her high school Driver's Ed class told her to keep her left foot pressed on the clutch to keep the gears from grinding. She experimented until something clicked that felt right. She eased up on the clutch and the car lurched backward.

Her attention had been so focused on gears and knobs, lights and heater controls, she'd forgotten she'd never driven by herself at night. Whenever she did drive alone, it was in daylight, to the grocery store, the school, Doc Boswell's or her parents'. A few times to her brothers', which was like going to her parents' since they all lived nearby on the same road. Those were the beaten paths of her daily routines, the memorized routes, the boundaries of her tame and sheltered world. Driving now into the dark was like being sixteen again and breaking the rules for the first time, the excitement and fear all mixed together. Pumped from somewhere other than her heart, currents of warmth surged through her loins and into her thighs, tingled through her arms and legs, her very fingertips that gripped the wheel.

She remembered the last time she'd desired Hap, a Sunday afternoon in late September. The kids had gone home with her parents after church. It was a day for turning off the air conditioner, raising the windows, and feeling the first cool breezes blow through the house, bringing with them the sounds and smells of the hills and the woods. All he had to say was, "Let's take a nap and cuddle." What followed were the fine, sensitive strokes of his hand along her back, a single touch when she rolled over, and she devoured him. When it was over, he dressed and went outside to work on the old car he kept in the backyard. For the rest of the afternoon, she lay there, drifting in and out of sleep, dreaming, wanting to touch the places that still ached. She'd never fantasized love with another man, much less allowed one to touch her, but when they made love again several nights later, it was Billy Ray's strong face she saw, his rough hands that roamed her body. In a fever of repentance, day and night she prayed. The more she prayed, the more the thoughts and images came, until she could no longer distinguish fact from fantasy. So, when Billy Ray put his arms around her one afternoon in the kitchen, the cry of the baby, like the blaring of an angel's trumpet, was all that saved her, both of them. As she stood quietly holding the baby, he promised not to come again unless Hap was there. The days and weeks that followed were worse than loneliness.

The road was in better shape than she'd expected. She was able to steer within tracks made by others. Occasional patches of macadam where the snow had melted slid beneath the headlights. Smooth white shapes swept by on both sides. Ahead, street lights of the town glowed like amber stars on a velvet sheet of night.

The only pay telephone, where there was light and people and safety, was at Johnny's One Stop near the center of town where the road dead-ended with the state highway. She recalled what her brother Frank had said once about men dressed in suits who use pay phones. "You can bet there's a man having an affair." No telling what people would say about a lone woman still in her Sunday clothes on a Sunday evening with a half foot of snow on the ground.

She approached the small store, lit up like a sale, and breathed relief. There were no other cars. The frumpy lady behind the counter would probably know her face, possibly her name.

She remembered to press the clutch with the brake as she came to a stop at the end of the long low-slung building where the pay phone was fixed to the concrete block wall. She found neutral and pulled the emergency brake. The car needs to stay running, she told herself. She rummaged around in her purse for two quarters. One to call Hap. She needed to call him first, to make sure he was not at home. For all she knew he was sitting at the living room window with his binoculars (the ones she gave him for Christmas and he never used) trained on Billy Ray's house across the road. Then the thought occurred to her he might be fool enough to camp out in his car near her parents' and follow her. He'd done that several times before they went steady and she was dating others, once even when they were engaged. Usually, he was drinking when he did it. She looked down the road behind her, but the only lights she saw belonged to houses and utility poles. Her fingers gouged deeper, touching everything in her purse but coins. In desperation she slipped a dollar bill from her wallet and walked under the dazzling awning lights into the store with the whole world looking on.

"Could you change this for me, please," she said to the clerk.

"Cigarettes or newspaper?" the lady said cocking her head to one side and passing would-you-believe eyes over her.

"Ah ... newspaper, please." This was the way men probably felt when they bought condoms, even married men.

"Must be something really newsy for a body to be out in weather like this to get a paper. Here's four bits. Sunday paper'll cost you that much now a days."

"Yessum. Thank you."

"Say, ain't you Lizzie Turpin?" The woman may as well have been the eye doctor looking into her with his little bright light. At least she didn't know her married name.

"Yessum."

"My daughter's Jenny Burleson. Y'all were in school together. Same class."

"Well, I'll say. Small world, isn't it?" and getting smaller, too, by the minute. That was all she needed. She struggled for a graceful way to leave quickly. "You tell Jenny I said hi. Well, got to get back before that baby starts crying again."

"So you got a little one, too. Jenny just had her—"

"Say, you don't by chance sell Pampers, do you?"

"Sure 'nough. Be right back." She walked quickly to the car and got her purse. The lady had the Pampers on the counter when she returned.

"That'll be nine fifty-six. Got to give the state it's share, you know, so's them politicians can fly around the world some more in their air-roplanes and bring another fact'ry to a little place like this, pumping ever' body up just to pop 'em bust."

"Yessum, reckon so." She gave her a ten and waited the eternity it took for the woman to punch in a hundred numbers on the computer register then another eternity for the little motors to spin and whir and click out the receipt. Just a few years ago, it only took two or three fingers pressing two or three buttons at the same time and "Bing," there was your change. She grabbed the bag and left before the woman could crank up her mouth again. She felt more than a little light peering into her as she walked past the newspaper machines to the telephone. A transport passed filling the night air with a roaring sound like judgment rolling down from the heavens.

She tried the first number twice, let it ring each time as long as she could tolerate. If Hap had been there, he'd surely have answered.

She stared at the phone a few moments, as though it were something to fear. Her teeth chattered, and her body shook from a chill whose source was a strange heat radiating from deep within her. Her finger quivered over the tiny silver tabs then struck them, one by one.

"Hello."

"Hap ... I'm sorry, Billy Ray. I had just dialed Hap's number. Guess I'm just nervous."

"That's okay. Where are you? I've been dying to hear your voice," he said.

"Me, too. I mean to hear yours. You can't imagine how hard this has been."

"I can. Now, where are you?"

"I'm at the One Stop. I told mother I was going to the house. Listen, Billy Ray, you need to know this. Hap is on to us. I don't know how. Just all of a sudden he came barreling into the house yesterday—"

"Just calm down, honey. Let Hap think what he wants. All that's important is that we be together. Drive on out and pull around back into my garage. You can cut your lights when you see the pine trees. The spotlights on the garage will guide you the rest of the way."

"Are you sure this is all right, I mean, that I won't be seen, we won't get caught? You sure it's safe?"

"As safe as shelling butterbeans. Now, come on."

"Okay. See you in a jiffy."

"Lizzie?"

"Yes."

"I love you."

She caught her breath and returned the words she was starved to hear, words that had become the wheels and axle of the universe, on which everything turned. "I love you, too," and hung up the receiver.

For a moment, she couldn't feel herself standing, couldn't hear the humming of the car engine behind her, as though she needed nothing else in the world. A sourceless wind would lift her and take her away.

"Miss Turpin!"

The voice from the doorway jammed her heart into her throat.

"Miss Turpin. I got an extra paper in here if the machine's all out."

8

Hap

By the time he reached the State Line, enough anger boiled inside of him to crack open a small mountain. The snow and ice saved a bridge abutment or two, not to mention several eighteen wheelers he considered ramming head on. He couldn't get up enough speed to knock over a mailbox. Three times, he stopped to winch cars out of ditches. The men wanted to pay him, but he refused. Love and being a good neighbor had nothing to do with his kindness. He needed to let off steam. For all he knew, the Good Samaritan had taken him over and been in his shoes. Once, he caught himself fantasizing Lizzie watching him, felt her feeling good seeing him helping others, until he pinched his finger on the winch and cussed her and Billy Ray and his mother for being where he was. His daddy caught a few words, too. Parents let you get tied to something and don't teach you how to get loose. He couldn't separate anger from hurt, didn't know whether to cry or hit the windshield again with his fist.

He passed the marker that said ENTERING TENNESSEE and turned in at a small grocery. The cardboard sign on the tree out front said BEER SOLD ON SUNDAY. Inside, a fat woman sat behind a long smooth counter. She was reading a newspaper and smoking a cigarette.

"A six-pack of Budweiser, please, ma'am."

Like it was a bother, she pushed herself up on her knees and pointed toward the rear of the cluttered store that smelled of old food and bologna and left over tobacco smoke.

He returned with the beer and added a Memphis paper.

"That'll be five dollars," she said. "Beer's four dollars on Sunday. Paper's a dollar."

He pulled a ten-dollar bill from his billfold and gave it to her. She rang up the purchase and laid a five on the counter.

"Thought you folks'd be closed today with the bad weather and all," he said.

"Nope. Ain't closed in twenty year." She showed no emotion and looked at him like he'd said something stupid. It was better than her saying nothing. He needed to talk to somebody.

"Wife just left me. Been married ten years, and she just up and left."

"That's 'bout half bad as me then." She blew a stream of smoke from the side of her mouth and crushed the cigarette in a jar lid beside the cash register. "Mine's been dead ten. Was married twenty."

"Gosh. I'm sorry."

"Needn't be. He was though. Ain't nothing better'n a woman relieved of a sorry man."

He wished he'd just bought his beer and paper and left.

"Again. I'm sorry."

"Again, needn't be, less you got something to be sorry for. World's full of enough folks

feeling sorry for theyselves, and most of it they borrow from somewhere's else." She looked at the six-pack he held in his hand.

He thought he'd left all the preaching he needed for one Sunday back in his mama's kitchen. "Yessum. Well, I'll be going. You have a good day now."

"You have a safe one. Them Memphis cops hard on a man drinking and driving."

"Who said I was going to Memphis?"

"'Cause you came from yonder," she pointed south, "you 'bout in Memphis and with what all you just done tole me, don't reckon you're going back real soon."

"You got that straight-ass right. No offense."

She nodded and lit another cigarette. He let the door slam behind him and opened his first beer where she could see him. He gulped half of it and added her to his list of sorry ass humans he'd cuss for the next twenty miles.

It was almost dark when he caught his first buzz, just past Collierville where the two-lane became four-lane. He was entering the city, the only one he'd ever known. Memphis. Huge. Sprawling, spreading further each year, spilling over the State Line into Mississippi, moving fast as kudzu.

He recalled the city as a child when he went with his mother on shopping trips. Memphis was huge then, but it seemed to be all in one place, crammed up against the River. Wide streets. Towering concrete rising from all sides. Signs, millions of them. Bumper to bumper traffic. Starting and stopping, starting and stopping. The smell of exhaust fumes and asphalt. He wondered then how the city moved and ran without crashing every second. Traffic lights. Who figured that out and pushed the buttons that made the lights change color? And all the people. Where did they come from? Where did they live? How would they get home safely, much less know how to find their way home? Did they have husbands and wives, brothers, sisters, front porches, grassy yards with lightning bugs, warm beds, night lights, Bibles with pictures and someone to kiss them goodnight? Memphis was just one city. Cities spread all over the world with cars, traffic lights, department stores, and jillions and jillions of people. How did God keep up with it? Hear all the prayers? Answer them? He was still asking as he took another swig of beer, thinking, "God can find you in the country. He can hear you there 'cause God made the country. He didn't make the city. Man made the city, made it 'cause it was harder for God to find him there." His foot pressed the accelerator.

The streets were almost empty. Only a few cars moved through snow that looked deeper. Than what he had left behind. It must have fallen harder and longer in Memphis. He looked at his watch. Five thirty. He left Hatchie at one. On a normal day he'd have made the drive in two hours.

From his shirt pocket, he pulled the small ad he'd torn from the newspaper he bought with the beer. He spread it carefully between his fingers above the steering wheel. In flashes from the passing lights, he caught glimpses of the girl's face. She was blond and beautiful. The words above her head said LOSE IT AT LULU'S. Lose what, he thought? Maybe your troubles. That was about all he had left to lose. Across the bottom of the ad it said HALF-PRICE WITH THIS AD. Below that an address—3900 Winchester. There were other ads in the paper, a string of them, some with prettier faces and several that said FREE ADMISSION WITH THIS AD. But he chose this one because he knew where Winchester was, just ahead, on the left.

Following other tracks in the fading sunlight, he made the turn from the four-lane onto a narrow two-lane road. He drove between unbroken rows of white fences and brick columned gates with the names of ranches arched above them in wrought iron. This was the fringe of Germantown, where the rich lived, where farms weren't really farms, the country wasn't country, and it wasn't city either. Though not this big and grand, the same thing was happening where he lived, just like his father said it would. "There'll come a time," his father said, "when people like us won't have property no more. Rich folks'll buy it all up just to look at it, not even work it, just put livestock on it and sit and look at it so they can count heads they'll pay somebody else to feed and feel richer and smarter and better'n ever' body else."

He took a long drag on his beer. Lizzie would sure enough love a place like one of these. Even if she didn't love him, she'd love it. Might even feel like loving him along with it.

He drove several miles before the road became four-lane again and the city began to flow around him. Strange looking modern churches. Shopping strips. Clusters of office buildings. Fast food restaurants and self-serve gas stations and cheap motels. Then a big mall that crawled with life. People doing their early Christmas shopping. They probably wouldn't be there if it wasn't for the snow, he thought. He and Lizzie brought the kids each year after Thanksgiving. They'd spend the day. The children would ride the carousel, pull them in and out of the shops, holler "look at this, look at this" a thousand times, sit in Santa's lap and tell him, not ask, what they expected to get, that, yes, they certainly had been good. Who'd take them this year? And watch them? He sucked dry one more can and opened another.

The warmth had moved from his insides to his head. His thoughts were beginning to get where he wanted them, floating. The magic was working. He'd joked with friends about his four beer personality, that with four beers he was the person he'd always wanted to be. After all, alcohol and guilt and shame can't live together in the same body. Earlier, when he'd stopped to pee on the side of the road, he considered what was leaving him and what would be taking its place, giving only a second thought to what would rush back in when he sobered, which was something he didn't plan to do, not for a long time anyway. Just keep the happy juice coming. Pouring in the future. Flushing out the past. Never stopping. Simple. Easy. Painless.

He was in the thirty-five hundred block and began checking the numbers on the store fronts. Lulu's would be in the next block. A fluttering pink and purple neon sign in the shape of a woman caught his eye. The large purple letters above her blinked LULU'S on and off.

Only a half dozen cars sat in the parking lot. He pulled in and checked his hair in the rearview mirror, pushed down the cow-lick in back, only to have it spring back. He licked his fingers and tried again. Next, he tried beer. To hell with it.

He paused at the door and thought about how he should make his entrance. Just walk in, take big strides like he came every night and knew everybody by name. That was how he bought his first beer when he was sixteen. It worked then. Not just with helping him buy the beer but getting rid of the scared.

He opened the door and took a long step into darkness and loud, twanging rock music. From the dark on his right came a gruff male voice. "That'll be five dollars cover charge."

He squinted and dug in his pocket for the five he'd never put back in his billfold when he bought the beer and paper then looked up and made out a shadowy bulk sitting in a glass cage. Through the small opening at the bottom of the glass, he slipped the five, along with the coupon.

"Two-fifty your change," the voice said then spoke to him like he knew this country boy was a first-timer. "Down the hall. Turn right at the end. Can't miss it."

His eyes followed a paneled wall lined with small lamps that threw pools of light over glossy photos of leggy nude dancers. His fingers brushing along the wall to guide him. He walked past the pictures to the corner and turned and, like the man said, he couldn't miss it.

In the center of a huge room was a raised platform ringed with black light neon tubing and four brass poles at the corners. A tall dancer wearing a bright red string bikini and bra and red spike heels was sliding around one of the poles. The flashing light over her head gave her a strange, jerky motion. As his eyes adjusted to the dark, he looked into deeper shadows along the sides of the room and made out cubby holes with couches. The rest of the room was filled with small round tables where single candles flickered in red and green colored bowls. Four men sat close to the dance floor. One reached up and slipped a bill under the string of the dancer's bikini bottom. She leaned over and kissed his bald head. He laughed and slapped his knee. The other men laughed with him. She dropped a finger onto his head and rotated her rear. The men laughed louder.

Several tables away, another girl snaked her body between the sprawled legs of a man wearing a beat-up Willie Nelson cowboy hat, blue jeans and clodhopper boots. The man was looking and grinning at the girl like any second she was going down on him. She wriggled in close to him then backed away when he reached for her.

Around the edges of the room, other bikini-clad girls balancing round trays one-handed above their heads slinked in and out of the cubby holes. He was watching them when he felt a hand on his elbow, and a low, husky voice whispered in his ear.

"How about a drink, love? You look thirsty."

When he turned his head, he was looking straight into a pair of cold blue eyes and smelling cheap perfume and something sweet on her breath that wasn't alcohol. He stepped back to get a better look. She was blonde and prettier than the picture in the ad. She wore a black sleeveless top and tight black shorts. He couldn't tell, but he bet her legs looked good too.

"Yes ma'am. Believe I will," wishing he hadn't said "ma'am." He looked enough like a country boy who didn't know shit from shinola about topless bars without announcing it.

She slipped her hand into the crook of his arm and squeezed. "Ma'am? Well, if that isn't sweet. Nobody's said ma'am to me in quite a while. You just find a seat, honey, and Maggie'll take care of you. What'll it be?"

"A beer. Budweiser'll do. In a bottle please." At least he knew what to ask for, which helped. Nobody warned him things would move this fast. He needed more time to be cool.

She smiled and winked and cocked her head back. "One Bud for my man." Her hand slid from his arm. Long fingernails traced a tingle that shot straight to his crotch.

He watched her walk away toward a bar on the far side of the big room. Yessir. Great legs. Long, sleek, thin at the ankles and set into black spike heels. Screwing shoes his buddies at the factory called them, only they used another word that where he came from was almost worse than the Lord's name in vain.

He moved to the right, along the wall where the couches were, and settled into one furthest from the light and action. Men from Hatchie came to places like this. He'd heard them talk about how their wives didn't mind as long as they looked and didn't touch. But most of them didn't tell their wives, just said they were in Memphis on business which was the other lie they told. The men he knew wouldn't have any business in Memphis. Word went around from time to time that important people were seen in topless bars. A county supervisor. Alderman. Once even a principal and a local preacher. Men probably gossiped more than women but they somehow kept it within their own circles.

As he waited, he watched the dancer and the men below her, their eyes bulging, their mouths hanging open like slavering dogs beneath a piece of meat just out of paw reach. The girl's gyrating moves traveled on the flashes of light, tracer bullets aimed straight at his soul. Through the blue smoke and electric air pieces of his life flashed before him—stolen glances at Playboy and Penthouse foldouts in the Corner Drug Store after ball practice; wanting Ramona long after their secret meeting at the shack. The faces of Lizzie and his kids came next, and a message pulsed in his swimming brain. *Get the hell out. Just get up and leave, Hap Pasley. You don't belong here.* But another message beat deeper, stronger.

The dancer unhooked her bra. A slow heat burned upward through his cheeks, into his forehead. In his whole life he'd only seen two women undress. His mother and his wife. His face felt the same then, like it was close to a hot fire. The dancer stretched out her arms and shook them. The bra slipped downward from a pair of small round breasts. He looked away a moment, then back. She rolled her hips in a series of bumps and grinds and swung the bra over her head, then tossed it into the lap of the bald-headed man whose face was tilted up into the bright light.

He thought about Homer before he's fed, looking up, his tongue hanging out. He guessed Homer had squirmed into a warm hole under the house. It'd be nice to need a place like that, safer too. Ole Homer had it made. A dog don't need much to make him happy.

The girl slid onto the floor, rolled a couple of times, moved her hands between her legs that scissored the smokey, light-struck air, then the lights around her went out. A D.J.'s voice came over a speaker. "OK, folks. Let's hear it for Sheba, sensuous Sheba. Next up is Dahlila, delicious Dahlila."

Softer music played, the kind he heard when he phoned the factory and the receptionist put him on hold. He became aware of an erection sliding down his thigh. "As a man thinketh," Jesus said. Just the thought did it, made you a sinner. If that were so (and it must be if Jesus said it), he was already branded for the herd that'd be raw-hided into hell. A man might as well go ahead and commit the sin. Jesus should've never said that. It was like giving permission.

He watched Maggie approach him, a bottle of beer on a tray balanced above her head. Swinging her body like a model, she sidled between the tables. His organ moved again. He was a condemned man on death row ready to feast on his steak before dying.

She set the beer on the low table and sat beside him, her knees tucked inward, almost touching his. Her eyes took him in, strange, searching eyes that stayed on his, bored through to what he was thinking. "Now tell Maggie what brings a fellow out to Lulu's on a night like this."

He'd expected something different, like maybe asking if he wanted a table dance for five dollars or putting her hand on his leg and telling him how hot and bothered she was and wouldn't he like to dance with her in a dark corner for ten bucks. He'd heard the most about those, where you got to touch them and rub up against them and get more than ten dollars worth from some. She didn't even ask for money after she put the beer down. It was just a slow night, he thought. Others sat alone, probably for the same reason he did. Made to sleep on the couch or in another room. Or worse, left by their women or kicked out. Why him? He'd heard about a quota girls in topless bars had to meet to keep their job. She'd move on soon. But he'd enjoy her as long as he could. He'd developed a sudden need for her. "I came 'cause there wadn't any place else to go." The words seemed to stay inside him, stirring a pool of sadness the alcohol couldn't move, just kept accumulating, like oil on water.

"What's your name?" She crossed her legs when she said it, and the point of her shoe grazed his leg.

"Hap. Hap Pasley."

"Hap?" She turned her head a little and said it again. "Hap. That's an unusual name. What in heaven's name does Hap stand for?"

Heaven's name. He wanted to think about that for a moment and where she came from with an accent like that, but her face was leaning into his, pressing for an answer.

"Henry Andrew Pasley. H-A-P. Hap. Parents couldn't agree on a name so they named me for my granddaddies. Nickname came later when they couldn't decide whether to call me Henry or Andrew."

She giggled. She looked out of place, giggling like a school girl with her hand over her mouth. He felt embarrassed that she was laughing at him. She moved her hand quickly to his arm and reassured him.

"I'm not laughing at you, Hap Pasley, but at me," she said. "That's what I should've been named, but not for any family."

It wasn't polite to pry into other people's lives, so he forced a smile and took a long swallow from the beer, the only cool thing in the building. The place was beginning to feel hot and stuffy. Cigarette smoke swirled around the lights like a muggy fog.

The D.J.'s voice came over the speaker again. "Delicious Dahlila, men. Here she is. Let's give her a loud Lulu's welcome." A few hands clapped. Across the room, somebody whistled. A tall black girl in a long white dress and white spike heels walked onto the stage. The lights went out. The place was suddenly dark. All he could see were the dress and shoes glowing purple under the black lights. A slow rock tune filled the air. The dress and shoes began to move. Maggie distracted him.

"Her name's not really Dahlila. It's Diane. None of the girls here use their real names, except me. It doesn't really matter. All of us should probably be named Hap." She dipped her head toward him and giggled again.

This time she was not being personal. "What do you mean?" he said.

"Hap. For 'happened.' Most of us just happened, somewhere, someplace," she flipped her hands back flat, Egyptian-style, "and ended up here for the same reasons you did. Just didn't seem to be anywhere else to go." She must have seen the screwed up look on his face. "I'm sorry. It just struck me as funny. No harm meant."

"None done." That was the coolest thing he'd said so far. She must have thought so too. She smiled and squeezed his arm and moved her foot inside his leg. He leaned back and pressed his leg firmly against hers, a test, to see if she'd retreat. She didn't. His next words came easy.

"Where're you from?"

"California."

"California's a long way from Memphis."

"And that's one long story, Hap Pasley." She looked over her shoulder at a burly fullback-looking man standing at the end of the bar. "Barney over there, the bouncer, likes us to keep circulating. But it's slow tonight. He won't mind. Where do you want me to start?"

"Why not with happened." They both laughed. Her hand came down with a dainty slap on his thigh, and the bulge under his zipper jumped.

Her leg slipped further between his as she nudged closer. She leaned forward, propped an elbow on a bare knee, a finger under her chin, and began.

"Let me see. I was born in California. I know that much. But I never knew my father. He left my mother when she was pregnant with me, and he hasn't been seen or heard from since. After I was born, my mother got jobs here and there. She was on a lot of drugs and couldn't hold a job for long, and we moved around a lot. 'A lot' probably says it all, should've been my middle name. As a child, I can only remember the name of one town. Indigo, a small town in southern California, not far from Palm Springs. But Indigo was a long way from Palm Springs, if you know what I mean. We're talking whistle stop."

This was the time to say something about Hatchie, but he kept listening.

"I started first grade there. Guess we stayed in Indigo longer than anywhere else, about five years. That's the longest job mother had, waitressing at a truck stop. She wouldn't have kept that one except she and the owner had a thing, and he let us stay free."

"You mean you lived at a truck stop for five years?"

"Almost. Except for the first three months when we lived in a cheap motel. Then mother met Danny, and did that ever start my life from bad to worse." She glanced over her shoulder again at the bouncer who was watching Dahlila.

"Danny started doing things with me, sexual things. I told my mother, but she wouldn't believe me. It was getting pretty bad, so I finally told my teacher. She called the Department of Human Services, and the next day there was an investigation. It was all nasty. Anyway, to make a long story short, and it's long, I was taken from my mother and placed in a foster home."

"Why didn't your mother tell Danny to stop or leave and go somewhere else?"

"That was the problem. She and Danny were in lov-v-v-ve, and she absolutely refused to believe me, said I made it up so we would move. She knew I didn't like living at the truck stop, much less Indigo. My first foster father fondled me, so I was moved to another foster home within six months. Those foster parents got divorced and I was finally placed with a set of parents that were really good. I guess I was twelve or thirteen at the time and thought my moving was over. I really lost count of the years. The

Rolands lived in Mecca which was not far from Indigo. They were an older couple, somewhere in their late fifties. They never had children. They truly loved me, and I grew to love them. I made good grades, became a cheerleader, all the neat stuff. When I was sixteen, Mrs. Roland was killed in a car wreck. They were on their way to Indigo, of all places would you believe, to a ball game to see me cheer. Mr. Roland got banged up, but he was okay. Human Servces said I couldn't continue staying with him, just the two of us. Rather than go through the pain of readjusting with new foster parents, I ran away."

He'd been watching her serious face, noticing the dimple on her left cheek when she moved her mouth a certain way, the small mole above her lips, the way she rolled her eyes upward every time something bad happened. Her last words caused something to click in his brain.

"Was it hard? To run away, I mean?"

"No sir. My time to be sweet and polite, Hap Pasley." She grinned. "It may have been one of the easiest things I ever did. I had really nothing to leave, so it was kind of like just walking away from a store you knew you'd never go in again because there was nothing there you needed, if you know what I mean."

He didn't. He sucked on his beer again and felt her watching him, trying to chase a sudden streak of pain, then she picked up the story again.

"I got lucky, hitched a ride on the interstate that took me to Phoenix. All I had was a beat-up suitcase with a few clothes, my curlers, stuff like that. I couldn't take much. Left a lot of things behind. There're those words again, 'a lot.' I did call Mr. Roland and told him I was okay and not to worry about me. He seemed to understand, but he broke down crying over the phone and that was about all I could bear. I never called him again. I stopped at a Methodist church in Phoenix and told the pastor I was trying to get to Little Rock, Arkansas. I had an aunt who lived there. It was kind of risky because I knew she might tell my mother. But when I told her what had happened, she vowed her lips were sealed."

"How did you get all the way from Phoenix to Little Rock?"

"The good pastor. He gave me money for a bus ticket. Even drove me to the station and saw me off. Called my aunt, too, and told her I was on my way."

"Shit fire." He'd held his wonder long enough.

"What's the matter?"

"And I think I got problems."

"I knew you did. Could tell it the minute you walked in. When you've done this as long as I have, you learn to read people pretty fast. Anyway," she took a deep breath and continued, "I stayed in Little Rock with my aunt and her husband. They were good to me. I graduated from high school there then came to Memphis three years ago with a girlfriend."

"You didn't run away this time?" He couldn't get running away off his mind.

"Nope. I still see my aunt every once in a while. She calls to check on me about every two months."

"And this is all you been doing for a living?"

"No way. I've been on a work-study scholarship at Memphis State for the past two years. Got one more year to go, and I'll get my degree in social work. With what I've been through it ought to be a Ph.D. I'm not going to stay stuck in a place like this like the rest of these girls. Some of them have been here eight, ten years. Most of them are prostitutes. It's all they know and probably ever will. I'm going to do something with my life."

She had no way of knowing she'd hit him where it hurt the most. He felt like an empty space where a balloon has been before it burst. "But you said you ended up here for the same reasons as the rest of them, me included." Maybe she told him that earlier just to make him feel better.

"I did. When we got to Memphis, this was the only job we could get. Jenny, my girlfriend, works over at Gidget's, another topless bar."

He'd seen that ad too.

"Now, Hap Pasley, I've been doing all the talking. Time to tell your story. First, let me get you another Bud." She didn't wait for him to respond but grabbed the empty bottle and was off. Striding away from him, she looked too good to be true.

Delicious Dahlila was winding down. Her dress was gone, a pile of glowing purple on the darkened stage. She wore only a string bikini bottom. He noticed a few more customers around the dance floor and thought about white men goo-gooing at a black woman, actually panting after her. They'd go back to wherever they came from and talk about the problems "niggers" cause the country. That was one problem he didn't have. He'd worked with blacks and took them as equals, which never helped him with Lizzie's folks. Dahlila was teasing the men with a scarf she whipped in their faces after pulling it through her legs. The D.J. did his usual, asked for an applause, and called out the name of the next dancer. Susan. Just Susan. She must not have a specialty, he thought, then wondered when Maggie would dance, hoping she wouldn't, or if she did, did it after he left, if he could. He'd face that later. She was back with his beer and a grim look on her face.

"Something wrong?" he said.

"It's that asshole Barney. He said I was spending too much time with one customer. I told him there were thirteen girls in here and twelve customers and if he didn't like it, he could take this bottle and shove it you know where."

His job. He'd almost forgotten. "Sounds like me."

"How's that?"

"'Cause that's what I'm gonna do in the morning when I go back to work. You know, pull a Johnny Paycheck."

"Pretty tough talk for a sweet guy like you."

"Oh, yeah?" He sat up straight, pumped his chest out and propped a foot on his knee. "Well, I can be tough when I have to."

"Al-l-l-l-l right!" She leaned over and tapped a finger on his chest. "Now, tell Maggie where this tough guy comes from and what he does when he's not out on the town." Her eyes were right up in his, unblinking, staring, looking strange again. A flutter rippled along the thin cords of her neck. He felt her hand on his thigh, almost touching him where he was hard and swollen. You weren't supposed to touch the dancers but she was all over him. He looked over at Barney who was looking the other way. She looked, too, and sat back, her hand still on his leg. He wanted to put his foot back on the floor, but was afraid she'd move her hand.

"I live in Hatchie, Mis'sippi. Work at a shirt factory in shipping. But not no more. Gonna tell that sombitch to shove it. Yessireebob."

"I heard that, Hap Pasley. But first, your life story. I'll bet it begins with Hatchie. That sounds close to hap-pen." They laughed together.

He began with yesterday and worked backward, drinking as he went. His tongue became heavy and loose in his mouth, and he needed it to lie down and let him get all the words in, but it wouldn't. She seemed not to notice, sat there and listened, her eyes steady on his. When he told about Lizzie leaving with the kids, she took one of his hands in hers and began rubbing his knuckles gently with her fingers. She kept doing that as he talked, rubbing his hands, squeezing every now and then, especially when he talked about his children. She leaned back when he spoke of Lizzie and Billy Ray and his mother, as though the fire coming out might burn her too. He unraveled twenty-nine years of hurt and anger he'd never known were there till yesterday.

When he finished, she got up and kissed him on the cheek. "You're a good man, Hap Pasley. You're just coming into your own, and it hurts like hell. Ole Maggie's got something that'll help that."

"Where you goin'?"

"My time to dance. I'm next up. But don't go way. I'll be back." He nodded. She didn't need to worry.

9

Liz

Her dress seemed to draw tighter at her waist and tug at her neckline. She knew the pounding inside was more than the leftover tremors from the embarrassment at the One Stop, more than the fear of being caught. It was the fear of not being caught, of turning herself loose in a darkness that received her all too easily, this lonely night that seemed to need her more than she needed it, the way it pulled on her.

Car lights approached in the distance. She was thinking right but turned left instead, a mistake of habit plus nerves. She could wait there until the car passed. No one would question her father's car in her own drive. It was the drive across the road she had to enter without being seen.

She saw no sign of life in the house on the hill. Against the lesser dark, where the cold purple sky touched the night-black land, she could barely make it out, a stranger shape than she remembered. The lights were off. But he'd have the lights off if he was watching.

"This is crazy," she said to herself. "I'm turning into a paranoid." She'd heard about paranoia on *Donahue*, that it came from guilt, which should qualify her for the State Hospital at Whitfield.

She could drive on up to the house and check on it, like she'd told her mother she would. That would be one less lie, one less layer of guilt she'd been stacking on like quilts. In the beams of the headlights, the snow looked deep, especially in the first swale where the narrow drive dipped before climbing. Deep ruts glared back at her. That's all she would need to get stucker than she already was. She talked to the air and waited for an answer. None came.

The lights finally passed behind her. She looked back. It was a pickup instead of a car. Her heart beat against the top of her head. If it had been Hap, he would've stopped. She was about to ease her foot on the clutch when she saw lights coming from the opposite direction. She had to wait again. If she got stuck now, how would she explain to a curious passerby she didn't need help. Maybe going to Billy Ray's would be easier, simpler. Her mother's warnings joined the other vibrations that shook her nerves to their limit.

This time it was a car. She watched its taillights disappear into the flat darkness. The highway was clear. She waited briefly, just to make sure, then released the clutch and pressed the accelerator. The wheels inched backward, spun a few panicky seconds then slid sideways back onto the highway.

In daylight, she could have easily spotted the entrance to the long gravel drive that cut across acres of fields before vanishing into a thick line of trees. Though they were neighbors, she'd been only once, to take a dish when his wife died. That was spring, two years ago. She recalled vague features of the house. A long low-roofed ranch-style type bordered by azaleas and daffodils and tulips. Bright pink thrift lined the walk to the front door. She gave her dish to a lady she'd never seen, mingled briefly with others in the crowded living room, and left. What to say to someone at a time of death had never been easy for her.

If darkness was not enough, the sameness the snow gave the land caused her eyes to strain along the shoulder of the highway. She spotted a place where tire tracks curved to the right, and she took it. The car plunged downward, its carriage drifting smoothly through the snow. For a moment she floated, as though on cushions of clouds, until effort was required once more to steer the car within the slippery white ruts, toward a bright light shining through the trees.

As Billy Ray had instructed, she turned off the headlights as she entered the trees. The spotlight at the corner of the double garage blinded her for a moment, then she saw him standing under it, waving her in. Nervously, she guided the car between his truck and a wall lined with garden tools and coils of orange extension cords and fishing rods. She heard a rumbling like thunder and looked back to see the garage door sliding down, as though they were being sealed off by some dark mechanical magic. Billy Ray had thought of everything, except how to calm her terror when the wide door finally clanged shut. For the first time in her life, she didn't know how to get out of a car.

She stared straight ahead. Her hands felt glued to the steering wheel. She barely heard the pecking on the window. When she looked, he was making a rapid turning motion with his fingers. Finally, he opened the door.

"Turn off the motor, hon. Unless you want the headlines in the *Bedford Sentinel* to read LOVERS FOUND ASPHIXIATED IN GARAGE." His smile looked strained.

She turned the key and held his hand as he helped her out of the car. Her hand still in his, she followed him through a laundry room. Beneath a rack of assorted coats and cowboy hats, lined neatly in a row, were pairs of boots and shoes, looking as polished and shiny as the day they were bought.

They entered a tidy blonde-tiled kitchen that smelled clean as a Pine-Sol ad on television.

"Who cleans your house?" She was thinking about the boots and shoes, too.

"I do. Anything wrong with that?"

"No. I just ... nothing."

The Formica countertops were spotless. Nothing was out of place except a Betty Crocker cookbook that lay open beside the stove. She had figured he was the kind who bought TV dinners at Jitney Jungle, whole stacks of them at one time. She had tried them once, when she was running a fever—meatloaf that turned mush in your mouth, hamburger steaks that tasted like chalk dust, fried chicken where the meat along the bone was still cold, even when she cooked them full power in the microwave extra minutes.

"Looks like you do your own cooking."

"Yep. Darn good, if I do say so."

She wondered if he did his own washing and ironing. His starched blue jeans were perfectly creased. The white shirt he wore, unbuttoned mid-chest, was wrinkle-less, even where the sleeves were rolled and folded across his tanned forearms.

He led her into a large den. At one end, a fire blazed in a massive stone fireplace the width of the wall. Above the mantel hung the portrait of a woman with soft features and strong eyes, a look that filled the room. Ivy Rather. She knew her only by name and face. They spoke cordially to each other, at the supermarket, ballgames, community functions, but that was all. She was a quiet woman who stayed in her own world and respected others.

"She was very pretty," Liz said.

As though it was something stricken suddenly with disease, he released her hand. She should have expected that, along with the silence that followed. For moments longer than earthly time, they stood and looked at the fire, the only sound and movement in the room, the only thing they could both look at that didn't hurt.

Her hands found each other behind her back, and she moved first, turning, observing. The wall opposite the fireplace contained an elaborate entertainment center complete with television set, stereo and speakers, surrounded by shelves of books, Mississippi State souvenirs (she remembered he played football there), several softball trophies, pictures of his father and mother and sister and her family. She knew his parents were dead and his sister was a teacher in Atlanta. Her husband worked for Delta Airlines. Their two children looked to be about the age of Ruthie and Kevin. On a polished cherry coffee table in front of a long black leather couch was an open gold-leafed Bible decorated with a bright red marker. The words on the pages were red, which meant Jesus had said them. Across from the couch were French doors that probably opened onto a patio where he sat each evening and watched the sun set over the rich bottomland that he plowed and planted and surely drew his pride and happiness from. His family cemetery plot was out there, too, further off, close to the river. Her mind that had brimmed and bubbled with fixing up the place and running it was as still as death, and as cold.

"Let me show you around," he said, clearing his throat.

He started with the living room and worked his way from there, commenting on pieces of antique furniture, where each came from, beginning his sentences with, "It," never "We." She followed closely into the dining room where he pointed to antique silver bowls and platters and pitchers in a glass-paneled china hutch. These were all "passed down." An antebellum story was behind the crystal chandelier that hung over the dining room table that was ante-bellum too, made of red oak, the legs hand-carved. A large oil on the wall opposite the hutch was painted by his grandmother. "She's buried in the family cemetery," he said, walking quickly past a curio cabinet that contained bric-a-brac and knickknacks, delicate glass and porcelain figurines that must have belonged to his wife.

He turned into a hallway that led to several rooms. The first was an office with a dark-stained desk and wooden swivel chair. An adding machine and typewriter were on the desk, and tiered above them were shelves of more books, most about agriculture and farming and the stock market, a few novels. She glimpsed an understanding of his success where so many others had failed. Her father and brothers never read a book, and they were just breaking even.

Three other rooms were bedrooms. One, a guest room, and one for the children they never had. He didn't say that, but she could tell by the bright colored balloons on the wallpaper. He merely extended a hand toward the master bedroom and called it that, like an afterthought, his voice lowered and eyes on the floor. It was the room he and Ivy had shared the ten years of their marriage, the place where they had tried to make a family, before something as sudden and deadly as a brain clot took her. She didn't want to look. She wondered how a man slept by himself after having a woman pressed closely to his side every night. That had to be the greatest frustration of all, unless it was lying inches from someone every night and wanting somebody else who was there when she closed her eyes.

"And that's it. The Billy Ray Rather house." His careful choice of words. House not home. He nudged her elbow, and she walked ahead of him back toward the den.

"Can I fix you something to drink?"

She knew he meant a soft drink or coffee or tea, but for the first time since she drank once with Hap, a good strong shot of bourbon would have helped. She picked a spot at the end of the couch nearest the fireplace and sat down.

"Just a glass of ice water will be fine." The warmth of excitement she had felt earlier was gone, replaced by an unfamiliar chill, but she was thirsty. "On second thought, just water. No ice."

He gave her a puzzled glance and went to the kitchen where she heard the methodical movements and sounds of someone at home. Hap didn't know the glasses cabinet from the trash bin under the sink. Her mind toyed with thoughts, of what she could bring to this world that seemed so self-sufficient. He couldn't bring himself coffee in bed in the morning. But he probably had a Mr. Coffee on his nightstand, one with its own alarm, the coffee ready when he woke up. He couldn't have supper prepared when he came in from the fields, then she remembered an orange crock pot on the kitchen counter. He couldn't massage his own back, but he probably had a Water-Pik shower head.

He returned with two glasses of water and napkins and coasters he placed side by side on the coffee table, next to the open Bible. He sat beside her, carefully positioning himself to leave space between them. She'd purposely chosen a seat that took her line of vision away from the picture over the mantel. No way she could avoid seeing the open Bible that lay before her, like a scarlet trap ready to snap shut on the first sign of sin. She didn't know whether to offer a quiet prayer of thanks or ask for forgiveness, or both.

He draped an arm across the back of the couch and leaned his head toward her. His hand was beside her cheek, close enough to touch her if she moved. Up close, he looked less like Chuck Conners, The Rifleman, which was who she'd always thought he looked like. The gap in his front teeth seemed wider, his complexion rougher, gritty. Unclipped hairs curled from his nostrils. His eyes jumped nervously then leveled out just beneath his upper lids. "We've both waited for this a long time, haven't we, Lizzie?"

For the first time, she felt his need for her, not that of a husband for a homemaker or wife, or even a companion, but of something simpler. He was managing the complexities of living. All she had to do was look around and see that. What she saw now in his face was a longing, an urge. It traveled on the musk-scent of his aftershave and heaved beneath his dark chest where a gold chain lay almost hidden under a forest of hair.

Quickly, she took a drink of water. It may as well have been bourbon, though the slow burn was all hers.

He must have seen and felt it, too. Like the fine edge of a feather, a finger traced a hot line down her cheek. "You seem to be somewhere else."

"I have been somewhere else," she said, studying the intensity in his eyes. "I'm trying to just be here. It's taking a while."

"Relax."

She could've done that if he'd just stopped there.

"It's just us. No one else knows you're here."

She smothered her first thought then gave it a little room to work itself free. "I feel like an intruder."

"There's nothing for you to intrude upon." He said it so unquestionably.

No, she thought. Just the ghost of a marriage that may have been dead and buried but resurrected itself almost everywhere she looked, as though the ghost-wife herself carefully planned it all before her death and waited in this sanctuary of the living dead for the first woman to enter so that woman could get her fill and see, then, if she wanted to stick around. Funny how death and corpses seem to somehow get the last laugh. Lizzie Turpin Pasley may as well be a Free Will Baptist trying to pray in a cathedral filled with idols of the Virgin Mary.

She had to challenge him, and her. "Billy Ray, tell me something. You ever thought of leaving this place?"

"Nope. Could never do that."

She started it. She'd finish it. "Why?"

"The land. It's a part of me." He leaned back and looked upward, as though at a vision on the ceiling. "It's the best addiction you can have, smelling the ground broken in the spring. Just something about it. I walk over it, the same places where my father walked and his father. You get a sense of being with them again, if you know what I mean, almost like a religious experience, and they're there, maybe kind of like Jesus on the Mount of Transfiguration, being with Moses and Elijah. I get high just smelling the soil, feeling it crumble under my feet, seeing the first green shoots of crops, not to mention everything else that's out here. Nature. Trees. Wildlife. The river. You know."

She knew. "Everything else" said it all.

"It's the feeling you belong somewhere," he continued, still looking up, absorbed in himself, completely unaware of the dream he'd just gutted. "Every man's got to have that."

She suddenly hated men, their insensitive conceit and over-sized egos. She felt like throwing the glass of water in his face and running out. Who did he think he was, this open-shirted, gold-chained, Brute-smelling macho lord of the land talking about this religious experience and coming on to her like she was a dog in heat and his dead wife practically sitting on the sofa with them? Like a big bird swooshing over her from the clear blue, her mother's words about weeds and swapping problems sailed down from some high place in her brain, down to where she could really see it now from all sides.

She twisted her anger in her fingers, where she could keep most of it down and let the rest out through her mouth, the part closest to her brain. "Here I am, Billy Ray Rather, about to leave one man tied to land that grows nothing, to join a man tied to land that seems to grow everything, including spooks, and I'm beginning to ask myself, where do I fit in?" She wished she hadn't said "spooks."

He looked like a man stabbed in the back as he jerked up, almost spilling his water. "Liz Pasley, what in the sam hill did I—"

"Maybe there's nothing anybody's not tied to and everybody has to somehow find their own hitching post." Any heat that had been anywhere else in her body she gladly welcomed to her face, where he could see it.

"Lizzie, I'm sorry if I—"

"I guess it would be kind of nice to be tied just to yourself. Then you could go anywhere you wanted to go and wherever it was would be home. Whoever said, 'Home is where the heart is,' was right, literally. Yours needs to be out there wallowing in your fields and backslapping haints. Mine's staying right here inside of me and going through that door." She pointed to the kitchen door and got up to leave.

He grabbed her by the shoulders. His pupils were tiny alarms ringing in sockets suddenly doubled. "Lizzie Pasley, I love you. You can't leave like this. Please. Just sit down a minute. I don't understand."

Emotions she had struggled to contain in the various compartments of her body—stomach, lungs, throat—had broken loose and were jam packed behind her eyes. She fell against him as his arms encircled her. Her body went limp against his as he pressed her closer, and she clung to him like a climber on a ledge. His body felt firm where hers was soft. She couldn't think, had no desire to think, only feel and in the feeling drift to a place she'd never been. His hands moved down her back and guided her closer to that place. She'd quit crying. Her eyes were closed, and she heard only the sounds of her own whimpering until they hushed on his lips as their tongues found and fought and probed for more. The floor was no longer beneath her, and something soft received her when his hand slid between her knees, and she opened her eyes and saw the ceiling lights like eyes glaring down from heaven, and she heard herself screaming, "No! No! No! Stop! Stop! Please, God, stop!"

10

Hap

A spring seemed to close his eyelids as he forced them open again. The red taillights of the Volkswagen in front of him looked smaller. He couldn't afford to lose her, not now. He slapped his face, twice, the second time hard so it stung. He looked at the clock dial on the dash. Three o'clock. She told him they closed early because of the slow crowd, or they'd still be there when the sun came up. He'd switched to drinking water, her suggestion, so he'd be sober enough to follow her when they left. That was her suggestion, too. She told him it was senseless trying to drive home that late and a waste of money to stay in a motel. Besides, she could use the company, which was a welcome switch, somebody needing him for a change. He needed anything to help him forget yesterday and stall tomorrow, which was bearing down on him like the last day of reckoning.

She turned left, off the wide, lighted streets. There the city seemed like any small town between midnight and dawn. Narrow streets. Big trees. Dark houses, a few with the porch lights still on. A stillness and emptiness that makes anyone awake and moving around at that time feel important. Tire markings in the snow were fewer there. People had stayed home today, been close, played in the snow. Thin tracks of a small sled ended at a front door, kept on going in his mind, painfully. Soon these sleeping windows would blink on. Behind them people would begin their day, people who knew what they were doing, where they were going, and why. Fathers waking children. Mothers cooking breakfast. Tables being blessed. Last reminders. Hugs and kisses. Goodbyes. The weight of his hurt tightened across his chest and closed in on his throat.

Sunrise three hours away and home four, if the drive back was anything like the drive up, and all he could do was follow someone whose last name he didn't know. He'd planned to walk through the doors of the shipping department at seven and tell his boss to take his job and shove it. He'd worked a hard ten years. Made production. Done overtime when told to. Never complained. Never missed a day. What'd it get him? A layoff that helped break up his marriage. No one would care if he didn't show up returning for work. He wouldn't even be missed. They'd just swing somebody in from packing which would create an opening there for another poor soul who needed a job because he couldn't farm and was tired of living on food stamps and wanted his pride back. Boxes of shirts with Pendleton and Duckhead labels would keep right on rolling down the line, to be shipped all over the country where rich folks would buy and wear them as though they were made in New York or Chicago or Atlanta and not in, God forbid, Hatchie, Mississippi.

Scooting and bumping over the snow, the Volkswagen looked like a small hooded sled guided by somebody who knew where she was going. He thought about her dance, how different she was from the others, like she was the star and the star got to keep her clothes on. All she took off was the scarf around her waist. She was like a swimmer in a cage of smoky light, her arms and legs carving and stripping everything from the air that was trashy or sleezy. No one whistled. No one yelled at her. They knew she was special. Too good to be true, a girl like that in a place like that, and she'd picked him.

He looked down to check the gas. He remembered he didn't fill up when he left. The needle was barely touching empty. He could go another twenty-five or thirty miles on a straight stretch, but they were cutting and turning through streets like they were cow trails, probably were at one time. He'd be lucky to get another ten. The speedometer was broken, had been for over a year. He'd promised Lizzie he'd get it fixed. Kevin almost drove him crazy asking questions about it on a happier trip to the Ozarks last summer. He thumped it one more time and saw the bobby pin in the empty ashtray below. Lizzie used it for everything except ashes. Neither of them smoked, a vow they'd made to each other on their honeymoon. He looked back over the wheel, for relief. His eyes caught a tiny pink slipper from a Barbie Doll on the dash, up against the windshield. He'd kept saving it for Ruthie, meaning to give it to her and watch her eyes sparkle. He couldn't run from family, not even in his truck. God, he needed to drink again. He moved his hand across the seat. One more, the last of the six pack. He popped it and guzzled.

Her right blinker again. He steered the pickup, following her, and prayed this was the last turn. Her left blinker answered. She pulled into a short driveway. He parked on the street in front of a simple white-shingled duplex with small windows and a double step to the door. She seemed the type that would live in one of those modern apartment complexes for singles he'd seen advertised in the Memphis paper, a country club world complete with swimming pool, sauna, tennis courts, exercise gym. He wasn't prepared for a low-rent duplex apartment squeezed in among smaller square row houses that looked alike, tired and rundown and shrubless. The snow probably covered grassless patches of lawns, too.

He opened the door. The windless cold braced his face. The chill brought new life to his eyes first then shook the rest of him wide awake.

She waved an inviting hand. "Come on in, Hap Pasley, before you catch your death." (His mother would've said that but would've called him youngun instead.) She looked out of place in her rabbit jacket and shorts. The snow all but swallowed her heels.

His first step toward her cracked through snow that had thawed during the day and refrozen. He spread his hands to catch himself.

From the front steps, she laughed. "Watered-down beer won't do that to you, Hap Pasley. You're just used to getting out of a pickup onto a hill."

He tried to laugh with her, but what she'd said hit too close to home. He straightened his back and walked to the door and opened it for her while she worked with keys.

Inside, a damp warmth that smelled of furnace gas relieved the cold. She flipped on a naked ceiling bulb, the first real light he'd seen since sunset. She was pretty in the shadows of the bar, but beneath the glare of the bald overhead she was beautiful. Her hair had a shiny, wild look. Golden strands spun outward as she twirled, hands out, palms up, like part of her dance.

"Ta-duuum. This is it. Maggie's place. Not much. But it works."

She walked toward a doorway and began taking off her coat. His eyes followed her long legs down to the heels that clicked across the wooden floor. From another room, she called back to him.

"Have a seat, Hap Pasley. Make yourself at home while I get us a drink. I could use one now."

His full name. All night she kept saying it, like she was stamping something in, or out. He wasn't sure which. Maggie was the only name he had for her. He kept wanting to ask her last name. But after the life story she'd told, he'd settle for Maggie. Nothing worse than opening a can of worms on your first date, which was how his insides felt. A few beers would calm that.

He looked around the small living room at pieces of used furniture that didn't go together. An old sleeper couch with frayed edges and swollen lumpy cushions. A ring-stained coffee table on a ragged rug. Two fat wide-armed chairs of different colors, brown and blue. Against the wall opposite the couch, on unpainted boards across cinder blocks painted black, a cheap stereo set, probably bought at a yard sale. Several empty LP jackets lay scattered on the plastic lid and floor—Bruce Springsteen, Johnny Cash, Willie Nelson, Alabama, Elvis. Nothing that described her, though all of them did perhaps. In a corner, a small TV with rabbit ears sat on a wooden box covered by a yellow sheet folded several times. Above it, hanging by corded rope, an airplane plant, its green shoots trailing over the TV screen. It could've been any living room in any house, lived in by anybody who'd shuttled from pillar to post most of their life with little to show for it. Nothing to suggest it belonged to male or female, old or young, white or black. No pictures of family or friends or trips taken. Nothing cherished. It looked and smelled old, old without memories, a place that might hold somebody long enough for dust to collect but nothing more.

He sat down at one end of the sofa and settled into a cushioned pocket that held his rear snugly. A spring pushed against an organ that needed no help, was already lengthening once more, uncurling like a growing sausage in his underwear.

She returned holding two bottles of Budweiser before breasts that appeared larger, firmer in the light. "Your reward and mine," she said, tipping her head to one side and grinning. "There's two six-packs in the refrig. No limits now. Enjoy."

She plopped down next to him then stood quickly. "That's an awful lot of light for one room." She flipped off the overhead and turned on a small shaded lamp hidden on the television behind the draping plant. Against the yellow glow of the lampshade, the plant looked like a huge spider. He'd almost forgotten.

She kicked off one shoe, tucked a leg beneath her and sat down beside him. Her arm brushed the back of his head as it came to rest on the back of the couch.

"Take off your boots, Hap Pasley. Relax. You look tense," she said and began massaging the tops of his shoulders with her fingers. A tingle worked its way through his body.

Except for the short time in Doc Boswell's office, for almost two days, he hadn't been free of boots, or clothes, or had a bath. "Better hold your nose. This may be strong."

"Listen, Hap Pasley. If you've got a smell my nose has never met, it'll be a first. Besides, it's kind of sexy." Her lips puckered swigging on her beer.

She probably had seen and heard and smelled it all. He took several swallows before wrestling with his boots. His feet came out with a soft sucking sound, followed by the smell. He pushed down his sock and checked his wound.

"My God, what's that?" she said.

"Black widow bite."

"It looks like a bullet wound that's gangrened. Think you'll be able to keep that leg?"

"The doc says I will. He warned me it'd look worse 'fore it looked better. The medicine he gave me has helped. But it's still sore. Hurts like hell just to touch it."

"A good slug of rye whiskey would take that out."

He thought a moment. That story he'd keep to himself. She'd think he was a wimp for sure, having to crawl under his own house to get his own whiskey.

"We just won't look at it," she said and winked.

He nodded, pulled up his sock, and finished off the beer which was giving him a second boost. Without asking, he got up and walked toward the door he guessed led to the kitchen.

"Now, that's what I like," she said. "A man who makes himself at home."

The last word hung in his hearing like a song in the air when the music stops, until he saw the kitchen. It looked and smelled like a crud zone. Dirty dishes, several days old, were piled high in the sink. Crumbs and scraps of dried pizza lay on a countertop. Diet Coke and Pepsi cans and soft-drink cups sat on top of a dark spot where something had been spilled. The lid of a Styrofoam carry-out box was flipped back. Inside, French fries and onion rings lay in pools of catchup and a Bacardi fifth bottle, maybe a swallow left in the bottom. Beside it, a saucer with an unfinished cigar, certainly not hers. He wondered how long it had been there and who it belonged to and why it was left and its owner was not there, and again, why he was.

The one-rack refrigerator held only a few items. On top was the beer she didn't lie about with some loosely wrapped cheddar cheese that looked old and cracked and a pint of milk in a wax carton, spout open. She probably used it for cream in her coffee in the morning. In the bottom were several eggs in a glass bowl, a can of instant biscuits his mother had called an abomination to cooking, a slab of country-cured ham in a sealed plastic wrap and a jar of orange- colored preserves.

He lifted a beer from a carton, was about to pop the top when he saw an opener lying next to the sink, the old "church key" type. He used it instead, to remember times on country roads late at night, full moons and the sounds of crickets, the warm humid wind across his face, the smell of freedom, long before he rededicated his life. What would it open tonight, he wondered? Or close? He chugged several long swallows.

When he returned, she was sitting in a sideways position, one leg dangling. She patted the cushion to finish the message.

He sat and gazed at a blank wall and thought unspeakable words while his mind groped for others. A Roman candle rode the curve of his cheek upward, looped, and fell, still afire. She did it again. This time her fingernail looped his ear. No one had ever done that to him. From the corner of his eye, he saw the blur of her face studying his and felt her breath. He felt his own speed up along with his heart that was pumping like a piston revving in low gear. The coiled heat in his crotch popped through the slot in his jockey briefs and found more room to grow.

"You love her, don't you?"

She might as well have tossed a firecracker into the best part of a wet dream. Something not connected with her touch burned his face. He turned and looked at the parted mouth where the words came from, at the sultry puffiness in the middle, thinning out to the corners. With the lipstick gone, worn away by the evening and the beer, her lips had a moist, natural gleam. Her tongue licked away a mustache of foam above her upper lip. The bulge in his pants drained. He'd heard about these women before, the teasers that get you all hot and bothered then pull the plug on you. Surely, she was not one of them. She didn't even tease with her dances like the others. She was too nice and sweet, sincere. After all, this was her idea. She pushed it. Surely she had a reason for saying what she did, which really didn't seem like a question the way she said it but something else that pried him open. When he needed them most, sometimes a few beers helped him find words to say.

"You oughtta be a shrink 'stead of a social worker." He felt his tongue thick and his words begin to slur and knew he was not far from crossing a line.

"I just might someday, but you didn't answer me." She shook her head backward, gathered her hair in both hands and piled it on top of her head. Gold loop earrings swung along her cheeks. He wondered how they could do that, earrings, make a woman look sexy. The danglier, the sexier. Lizzie never wore them. He imagined them on her. Dangling earrings. High heels. Tight shorts. Tight blouse.

"Yep."

"Yep, what?"

"I still love her. But you're a educated woman. You ought've known that. Can't stop loving somebody," he snapped his fingers, "just like that."

Her lip poked out. She looked hurt, like he'd insulted her.

"Well, when your..." She paused and looked away.

From the side, he watched her eyes struggle, like there was something behind them needing to get out, something old, packed deep.

She glared back at him. "Nope. You're right. Stupid question. Sorry I asked," she said and ran her finger again around his ear and down his cheek, touched the corner of his mouth. "We won't talk about *her* anymore." She bore down on the word her then the bottle, finished it off before setting it down hard on the coffee table. "How about some music?"

"Yeah, why not." He needed to feel different. She did, too. Something was simmering inside of her, and Lizzie was back working on him. Music with a good buzz had a way of making him feel someplace else, like he was in the song and doing everything the song said, even when he didn't listen to what the song said, even if there were no words, just the music did that, as though is possessed an energy all its own, carried him away.

She sorted albums, removed jackets, studied labels. When she bent over, her shorts tightened around her rear. Her blouse pulled loose from her waist, and he could see a waist line of pink panties. Warmth stirred in his crotch again along with the question he kept trying to drown: How could he still love the woman who left him and want one whose last name he still didn't know, and why didn't he care?

She placed a thick stack on the turntable. A click and a slap followed. Elvis dropped into the room singing "Heartbreak Hotel."

"That one's for you," she said, "so you can get *her* out of your system. The next one's 'Baby Let's Play House,' if you get my drift." She was sounding less and less like a social worker and with one leg bent, her hands cocked on her hips, looked like a drum major before the whistle blows and the band starts to march.

She'd just said they wouldn't talk about *HER* anymore and now she was aiming *HER* straight at him. Drift was the right word all right. He got hers. It was his he was worried about. The tricks memory plays, at the oddest times, especially when you're drinking and listening to music and neither is helping much. Like an old dream he saw them, him and Lizzie, a summer night before children came along, fishing on the Hatchie River when they untied the rope and let the boat float with the moon-bleached slow water, escaping dark shapes that seemed to reach for them, mindless of how far they went or where they ended up, laughing and giggling like drunks. One of those moments in time that, when you think about it, reminds you of the best you had, enjoyed the most, but didn't know it at the time, that you can't ever make happen again. Drift. His memory fought back through ten years of marriage that had drifted. What happens to a man and woman that don't play together any more, that let kids and jobs and in-laws come between them, drifting further apart so a Billy Ray can step into the picture.

"Down the end of lonely street..." Elvis sang, in that white man's voice sounding like a black blues singer. "You make me so lonely, baby, you make me so lonely. You make me so lonely I could die."

This was the terrible drift of facing yourself with no one else in the boat to help you. Maggie was paddling her own. He fought the hurt in the bottom of his throat and tried to keep it there.

"Hap Pasley! You didn't hear a word I said." She said it in a tone of voice women use for a good-ole-boy slap on the back.

"Yep. Ever word. You AND Elvis."

"Too much, huh?"

"Maybe."

"Sorry."

"No problem," he lied.

"Want me to play something else?"

"Yeah. As long as it's not 'Love Me Tender' or 'Baby Lets Play House.' How about 'You Ain't Nothing But A Hound Dog?'"

He didn't mean it to be cute but it came out that way and they laughed. His came from deep inside, the escape of a gusher kept so long pent up it could've easily been a cry.

"You got it," she said, going into action again with the records. This time she turned down the volume before coming back to sit beside him, closer. "Now, let's talk about that hound dog."

He thought she meant Lizzie, but the way her eyes were back to that strange stare he couldn't figure out, moving over his face as though searching for a soft spot, a place to enter, he knew it was him she meant. He wanted to help her, and him. Its hinges greased with beer, he swung a barn door wide open.

"I'm scared to death of being alone."

Her face turned serious. Her eyes lengthened, almost to a squint, the way eyes will before a cry. She reached for his hand and held it. "I know. If it makes you feel any better, most people are." Her voice thickened. "But what they really fear is being LEFT alone."

"Thanks a bunch. You just doubled my scare."

"Sorry." She leaned back and looked surprised. "Guess I need to work more on my active listening skills."

"Your what?"

"Active listening skills. Tuning into what the other person is feeling then giving it back to them so they understand themselves better. That's what we're learning in my counseling class."

"In that case you get a A plus. Your ears may as well have been cross hairs on a scope, holding steady on dead center. I got plumb forsook." He wasn't even thinking the next words that popped out. "You ever thought 'bout killing somebody?"

Her face changed again, suddenly, her voice, too, leveling into a low mean tone. "Yeah. Many times. The same person, over and over." Her eyes narrowed. He thought he saw what he'd seen moments earlier there, struggling. "Killing him wouldn't be enough though. I'd dig him up and do it again and again. Nothing quick but something slow, so I could watch him suffer." She ground out the words with her teeth. "Hear him cry out for help then let him have it again." The tiny muscles along her jaw jumped and rippled. "Just to watch him pay." Her eyes narrowed even more as though he was the one being singled out. He wondered what nerve he'd touched to change her so, to bring on a look he'd never seen before. He'd seen hate, but this was way beyond that, and he was in its way.

"Who in the hell you talking 'bout? I was talking 'bout the no good sonofabitch who's been seeing my wife," he said before downing more beer, keeping his eye on her while he chugged.

"Can't any sonofabitch top my ole man. If I ever see him—no, if I as much as learn his whereabouts, he'll pay. I'll make him pay for leaving me and my mother." She was grinding her teeth and popping her jaw muscles again. "For every mile of road, every hungry and sleepless night, every lecherous hand that's pawed my body, that worthless sonofabitch'll pay." Then her face turned back sweet again, a paste-on smile. "I don't want to talk 'bout it anymore. Let's talk 'bout something else," she said, killing her beer.

"Suits hell outta me," but he was thinking about the sudden loose screw that was rattling her brain and where he was going to sleep and the fear of waking up sober with a hangover in a strange place that'd be emptier than the house he tried to burn and left. "Don't you have classes today?"

"It's exam week. Don't have my first one for two days." She squeezed his hand and gave him a back-to-normal smile. "I'm looking forward to cooking breakfast for somebody other than myself and enjoying him as long as I can."

Across the room, the stereo whirred and clicked. Another record dropped, one of Willie's. He was singing about all the pretty girls he'd known. Those were words he needed to catch and ride. What Maggie had just said to him kicked in with the beer. He forgot her outburst and loose screw and placed his hand nervously over hers and did something he hadn't done in ten years, not even with Ramona Waycaster. He kissed a woman other than his wife. She placed a hand behind his head and kept him close. Her lips and tongue moved on his like something wild and starved. He tried to pull back, but she pressed harder, sucking his tongue into her mouth like she'd swallow it, roots and all. He heard himself groan, and she finally let up and leaned back. Her eyes were closed. In the dim light, the dreamy expression on her face looked like the face of somebody drugged. Without opening her eyes, she pushed herself on him, and they fell backward on the couch. Her mouth was on his again. She shifted her body until she was on top of him, moving against him, out of control. His brain was fogged over with beer, and the ceiling was turning. He didn't resist as she clawed at his buttons and belt and zipper. Before he knew it, her rough hands had guided him into her and she was riding and whipping him like he was a runaway horse, something to be taught a lesson, screaming words of filth he'd never heard come out of a woman's mouth.

When it was over, she slipped away quietly, and sleep, like the beginning of a long, wet cloud, spread its cool softness over him.

11

Liz

She remembered Billy Ray hollering after her, over and over, "I love you, Lizzie, don't go," and racing the motor so the car would make it up the grade to the highway without getting stuck, and the house still dark on the hill, but she remembered little else. Her forehead was sore where it lay across the hard steering wheel. She raised up, unsure of where she was. Through sheets of tears, she'd turned onto the first road she came to and pulled over onto the shoulder. By the tilt of the car, she knew she was lucky to be upright. She switched on the overhead and looked in the rearview mirror. Her face was clawed with mascara. She rummaged in her purse and found a tissue. Her hand still shook as she dabbed around her eyes and erased the black smears and streaks. She looked at the wrinkles in her dress and tried to smooth them with her hands, thinking all the time her mother couldn't see her like this. She turned off the light and looked through unwashed windows into a murky darkness where no light shined. Her hand fumbled along the dash for the keys in the ignition. She pressed the clutch. The key turned easily, the motor started, and she touched her toe lightly to the gas. She'd never driven in snow but knew to go slow and keep the gear in low. The car moved a few inches and stopped. The tires spun in the snow. She tried again. The tires whined again.

The scare she felt was different from the one she left behind at Billy Ray's. This was one she could pray from.

"Dear God," she whispered with her head down. "This is Lizzie Turpin Pasley, in case you might've forgotten. I'm going to make this real simple. No ifs, ands or buts about it. Please help me get this car to moving again."

She gave time for the words to be heard and more time for a heavenly hand to touch earth in the right place. Once, she had watched her father get his truck unstuck from a mud hole in a pasture. Using the low and reverse gears, shifting his feet between the gas pedal and the brake, he lurched the truck back and forth until it eventually rocked free. She pressed the clutch and shifted into reverse. The car jumped backward. Her left foot still holding down the clutch, she shifted into low and the car moved forward. She repeated the action several times. The car was rocking, and she was asking and thanking God at the same time while it rocked. Then she pressed firmly on the gas, and the car moved forward, slid sideways and the tires spun again.

She was utterly alone in country she was supposed to know. She was ready to have it out with God and thought of the worst thing she'd ever done which was worse than what almost happened at Billy Ray's, yet nothing this bad had ever happened to her. She could pray again but doubted there'd be anyone out there who'd care to listen. So she talked softly to herself. "Stay calm. Just stay calm, Lizzie. Help can't be too far away." She recalled something she saw on television about not leaving your car if you were stranded in snow. She could at least open the door and look around.

The door was heavy because of the angle of the car on the sloping shoulder and made a loud squawking sound as she pushed it back with her foot. Using the steering wheel for leverage, she pulled herself out. The wet chill of the snow cut through her shoes. A light breeze blew cold against her face. She checked the car's position. The rear had slipped further down the embankment. If she tried again, she risked slipping further down the bank into God only knew what, making it harder to winch out if and when help came.

She tried to get her bearings. On her left, a silver glow hung over a long bulge of inky horizon. That had to be the lights of Hatchie. That was north.

Behind her was west and the highway, a good mile back she guessed. She was crying so hard she paid no attention to how far she drove before she stopped. She tried to remember which direction she turned when she sailed out of Billy Ray's drive and thought she might have turned right in her confused state of mind instead of left which would have been toward Hatchie. She was thinking about Hap and trying to go a direction where her headlights wouldn't hit the house. That would've been right. If she took the next left, that would've put her on a road she knew only too well.

Toward the east, in front of her, a distant light, faint, winking through the trees. She held her breath. Her heart beat loud in her ears, and she breathed again. If she was where she thought she was, and she probably was, she knew the house. There wouldn't be another between them and not another beyond it for two miles and behind her nothing but the state highway. She leaned into the car and switched on the overhead and looked at her watch. Almost eleven o'clock. Her mother would be having a conniption fit. She flipped off the light and stood again in the dark cold. She stepped up and down to relieve the pain that was bleeding into her feet from the snow and slapped her arms against her side. Above her, stars glimmered in a sea of sky where small puffs of clouds looked like islands, their shores outlined by light from a bright chip of moon. The story she would tell began to unravel in her mind.

She reached back in the car and got the keys from the ignition and grabbed her purse. Placing her head through the strap of the purse so she could put her hands in her coat pocket, she began walking. She kept her eyes moving between the light and the road which was visible only as a wide chalky path whose fuzzy boundaries faded into blackness. She thanked God for the meager moonlight. Her feet were beginning to feel brittle, as though they might break if she tripped. But her head was hot with a rush of energy and as long as she kept her thoughts on the house ahead, the rest of her body didn't seem as cold. Hap might be there. The best that could come of that was he would believe her. His mother was another matter. She was used to lies, could pick them out if they were blond fleas on a collie.

The light came closer and vanished and told her she was nearing the front of the house which was still off the road another hundred yards. She reached a shadowy object on the side of the road she knew to be a mailbox and turned into the narrow drive, but she had to feel with her feet in the thin moonlight. She'd been over the drive countless times she wished she didn't remember, but now memory helped guide her. The large house she'd been able to make out in the dark from the road was hidden by thick growth that tunneled with a dim hole of lesser dark at the end, which she kept her eyes on. Her feet burned, and the pain had moved into her calves, and her face stung in the slightest breeze, but she was not far from warmth and a telephone. She wondered about her mother and hoped she'd not alarmed her father or called the sheriff's department. She was capable of doing both, and did once, when she and Hap were out too late one night on a blanket in a pasture just a stone's throw from her house.

No bird or animal or insect sounded in the wooded corridor dark as Egypt. The only noise was her breathing and the crackling of frozen trees in the wind and an occasional soft splattering of snow falling through limbs to the ground. In warmer weather, a million stirrings would have scared her silly and sent her into a panic. The fear that shook her now lay ahead, in the house.

At the end of the draw, the night appeared brighter and the house loomed on the hill against the purple sky. She walked where she remembered the drive curved upward into the front yard. Her eyes were better adjusted to the dark, and she could make out porch and columns and steps. Her feet carried her on until she came to the bottom of the steps, to an urn where she leaned briefly to catch her breath. Holding fast to the wooden railing, she continued up the icy boards. At the top, she stopped to catch her breath once more. Her feet were numb, and she noticed the pain had stopped there but burned still in her ankles and calves. Trembling, she approached the door and knocked on the facing and waited. Her knuckles hurt from knocking. Her heart was banging against her ribs. Her breath was short and panting. No sound came from within the big place. No sight of movement through the long narrow windows down the side of the door. Her knuckles still sore, she knocked again. Waited again. Nothing. She opened the screen door and tried the knob, and the door cracked opened. Mama Pasley never locked the door, she remembered. She called her name, "Mrs. Pasley."

Louder. "Mrs. Pasley!" A sliver then a band of light fell across the living room floor from the dining room and the shadow of a person moved across it until the shrunken outline of the woman stood in the archway of the dining room and said in a sharp voice, "Are you friend or foe?"

"This is Lizzie, Mama Pasley."

"Well, for heaven's sakes, child, come on in and turn on the light. I thought I was being robbed."

She flipped on the switch beside the door. Hap's mother stood in her nightgown with a shotgun cradled in her arms.

"I hope I'm a friend, Mama Pasley, but I wouldn't blame you if you thought I was a foe."

"Pshaw. You're my son's wife, ain't you? I ain't gonna shoot the wife of my son even though I oughtta take a horse whip to both of you younguns. Come on in. You look like a icicle 'bout to break."

Lizzie followed her through the dining room into the steamy kitchen.

"Take off that coat and sit in front of this fire. Didn't see no car lights. Didn't know what kind of devilment was on my porch."

"I think my feet are frozen, but I need to use your phone first."

"Well, go ahead. You know where it is. In there on the table by my bed."

"Yessum."

She walked carefully across a floor that creaked as though the house was settling again on its foundations. She crossed the hallway where a cool draft felt good and entered an even cooler bedroom that smelled of quilts and facial cream and old age. The only light was a small lamp on a nightstand beside an antique spool bed. The black telephone was the old circular dial type, the kind that gave you time to think while you dialed.

Her mother answered in one ring.

"Mama, this is—"

"Lizzie Turpin Pasley. Where in tarnation are you? Your dad and I've been worried sick about you."

"I'm at Mrs. Pasley's. I can explain later."

"I've rung your house for the past two hours, and no one's answered. We just knew you went off in a ditch."

"I did."

"What? You all right?"

"A little froze but all right. I'm thawing out." With the heat in Mrs. Pasley's kitchen, melting was more like it, she thought.

"I'll send your dad in the pickup. It's got a winch."

"I hate that, his having to get out in this cold and all, but it'll take a truck with a winch."

"Well, how'd it happen?"

"I'll tell you later, Mama. The car is between the highway and the Pasley drive. He'll see it. It's not all that bad."

"It's bad enough. Eulice!" She shouted. "It's her." Her father was probably still asleep in his recliner. With Carson not airing on Sunday nights, nothing would awaken him. "He'll be right there, hon."

"Thanks, Mama."

"What've you heard from Hap? He there?"

"No, Mama. I don't know where—I don't know." But she knew he wasn't at home. He'd have answered the phone.

"Land's sakes. You'd think he'd be at home."

"Yessum. You'd think." Across the hall, the kitchen was too quiet. "Mama, I'll see you shortly. Bye," and hung up before her mother could continue.

Somewhere in the room, a clock ticked. A drip from a bathroom faucet answered. The kitchen was otherwise without sound, as though it were part of the frozen world outside. The easiest part was over, the hardest about to begin.

Her mother-in-law sat at the small table staring at the wall with a look that could have held a picture. Her mouth looked like an old scar where stiches might have been once. Lizzie thought of the scars it had left on others. Then Mrs. Pasley's eyes turned from the wall and cut on her.

"Well? They a comin'?"

"Yessum. My daddy's on his way."

"Good. I need to get ome sleep. Go ahead and take them shoes off and warm your feet in front of the heater. Stove's 'bout out."

She pulled a ladder-back chair from the table and sat in front of the heater. Its bumpy panels glowed pink and orange behind the blue flames.

She kicked off her heels, pulled off wet hose and draped them across the back of an empty chair. Against the warmth of the heater, a different pain returned, one that was sharper and deeper, bone deep. Her skin began to burn. She scooted back from the fire, but the burning increased. She gritted her teeth and rubbed her red feet with her hands and wondered again what she'd done to deserve this. She was thankful Mrs. Pasley was behind her and couldn't see the tears.

"It'll burn awhile while it thaws. You prob'ly come close to being frostbit," Mrs. Pasley said.

Without turning, Lizzie nodded and kept rubbing her feet. If the woman only knew what else she came close to. She'd give up her feet any day before she gave up her soul. But she'd have never known that before tonight.

For a long time, the only sound in the sultry room was the steady loud whisper of the gas flames from the heater. Moisture beaded and ran in slow crooked streams on the smooth blank wall she faced. Her throat was dry, and she wanted a drink of water, but that meant disturbing a patient silence that protected her. Surely, her father would come there first before pulling the car free. Surely, he knew to do that. She was hanging on those thoughts when the voice behind her cracked the long quiet.

"Hap says it's another man."

She'd prepared herself, but the words still came, without warning, like a rifle fired at her back while she nursed a pain worse than childbirth. Hell couldn't be a hotter place or the devil a worse punisher. She longed for the snow and the cold dark and told herself if she ever stepped back into it again, she'd have paid for all of her sins and be free to start anew. That was the quick half-prayer she said to herself before she answered.

"So, Hap's been here. Is he all—"

"I said he said it was another man."

She turned around and met the fierce stare that awaited her, the boiling eyes in the bleached doughy face that looked her up and down like a criminal in a lineup.

"Mrs. Pasley, that's not the reason Hap and I are separated."

"Left. You left him."

"Separated."

"Left. He said you just up and left."

Even in the strangest of families, blood runs thicker than water. She knew not to argue with her. "It's been building for a long time."

"But you left him. He didn't leave you. No Pasley'd up and leave their family."

She prayed for the sound of a motor, a flash of headlights through the windows, any sign signaling her father's arrival in the front yard. All that came to her was a thought, but it might get her past the next minute. "If that's so, Mrs. Pasley, then where is your family?"

The thin body of the woman stiffened. Her neck straightened, and her head shook with her voice. "They're all together, thank you."

"Together hundreds of miles away from here. Except Hap, who might as well be hundreds of miles away, from you and me." She wanted to say Mrs. Pasley drove them away, but she wouldn't say that until she was safe in her father's truck with the window half up and the doors locked.

"Don't matter where they are. They're still families. There ain't nothing sacred left in this country anymore but family. And it takes two people to unmake a family."

"It takes two people to make a family, too."

"He was tryin'. Maybe not hard enough, but he was tryin'."

"I do give him credit for that."

"Give him credit?"

"Yes."

"Give him credit, you say. That's all you give him?"

"No. Not all."

"He provided for you and the kids. You had a roof over your head. Food on your table. Clothes. Respectability."

"Respectability?"

"Respectability. That's what I said. You lose that, and the rest don't mean much."

She saw her simple logic and where she was going with it. "I don't think anybody's lost any respect."

Mrs. Pasley didn't respond.

"We've both shown respect for each other."

Still nothing.

"We've never done anything to intentionally hurt one another."

"'Cepting your leaving. Folks won't look kindly on that. Kids won't neither when they grow up."

"I think my children love me and always will."

"Ain't got nothin' to do with love. We're talking 'bout respect."

"They'll respect me."

"You just wait."

"I intend to."

"They'll come to you askin' why their daddy ain't there."

That comment ushered up another thought that might buy another precious minute. "Just where is Hap? That's how come I'm sitting here right now half frozen, trying to find him to see if he was all right."

"Hmph," she grunted. "Likely story. 'Cept for the froze part."

"As likely as not. Why else would I be stuck near midnight on Sunday in snow and ice on a road in front of your house?"

Silence.

A headlight beam passed across the window. A horn honked.

She began putting on her shoes. They were damp and cool and felt soothing around her feet that were almost back to normal. "My daddy's here, Mrs. Pasley." She felt no reason to call her Mama anymore. "I need to go and you need your sleep. But before I leave I'd like to know where Hap is, if he's all right."

"Got no idea." The sharpness in the voice was gone, the eyes blinked slowly. "Left here mad as a hornet. Didn't say where he was headin' to."

She could imagine. He'd caught the other side of her wrath, hotter no doubt than the in-law side. She lifted her hose from the back of the chair, slung her purse over her arm, and made a move toward the dining room door, then stopped.

The old woman sat motionless in her chair and stared at her hands that lay on the table wrapped around empty space but shaped for prayer.

"Mrs. Pasley, you can tell him I came ... but I'd rather you didn't."

Mrs. Pasley looked up from her hands and nodded sleepily.

Outside, the cold air brought relief. Her father was no different from any other time when he knew more than he let on he knew. He said nothing as she entered the truck. They stopped where the car hung on the side of the road like a lame animal. She got in and turned the steering wheel in the direction he told her. He was a bent figure in the dark, connecting the chain from the winch to the front axle. When he signaled with his hand from the window, she started the car, listened as the tires spun briefly, then said "Thank you," to the air as the car pulled free.

She followed her father as he turned right onto the highway that passed between her house and Billy Ray's. She wouldn't allow herself to look and kept her eyes on the taillights ahead, two red eyes looking back at her out of the night.

Wherever Hap was, she hoped he was all right, though she wouldn't tell him that, not in a million years. If he talked to his mother, she'd probably tell him anyway. Blood does run thicker than water. So, it really didn't matter, this private part of herself she felt she needed to guard, and for reasons she couldn't name. Far better for him to think she was out looking for him than know she drove to Billy Ray Rather's and almost threw her soul away. That was between her and God and when she could think straight again, she'd talk to Him about it. After all, He did hear her. She had survived Billy Ray and her mother-in-law and the car was unstuck. With all the confusion going on in her mind, that much she did know. Where her life went from here, she had no idea. She couldn't go back, and she couldn't go forward. It would take some doing for God to get this unstuck. She certainly couldn't.

The glowing hands of the clock on the dash pointed to half-past midnight. Another wave of heaviness swept through her. For now, a bed and time to sleep would be an answer enough to prayer.

12

Hap

Pushed from behind by a strong hand, he was riding a runaway sled from the top of a high airy hill, sailing through blurs of dark clouds and huge dark rocks down a snowless rocky slope that had no bottom when something wet touched his cheek and a woman's voice said, "Good morning. Rise and shine." A faint perfume from the night mingled with smells of ham frying and freshly brewed coffee. He blinked into bright sunlight that shot through two bare windows above him and fired a blaze in his head.

"Where am I?"

"You're at Maggie's place. Or don't you remember." His eyes cleared, and he saw her and remembered the worst. She stood almost over him with her hands on her hips. She wore a black jogging suit with M.S. TIGERS in gold letters across the front. Her hair was pulled back tight in a ponytail, and she was smiling. "I hated to wake a face that looked like it was in a wonderful place having a grand time."

"Wherever I was, I was moving fast." He didn't tell her it was hell he was headed for. She might think she'd saved him when for all he knew she belonged to the hand that pushed him. That part of the night flashed before him again and a wave of guilt swept upward through him.

"Well, slow down and stop for breakfast."

He sat up and pinched sleep from the corner of his eyes. "What time is it?"

"Almost noon."

"Noon?" He scrambled for his watch he'd laid on the floor. "Oh, no."

"Oh, yes. Remember. Some foreman in good ole Hatchie, Miss, will be on an examining table with something stuffed up his ass."

"That's not funny. I want to tell him in person."

"Still can. There's a phone in the kitchen."

Phone. He needed to call home. He'd already missed the kids. They'd be in school. His mother didn't deserve to know though she probably had the highway patrol out looking for him. A call to Lizzie would be wasted and only upset him again. He'd wait until school was out. The kids needed to know he was okay. Everybody else could guess. "Never mind."

"Good. Let's eat. I'm starved. Bathroom's around the corner to the left."

He gagged on the word starve, but he did need to pee. After relieving himself, he washed his hands and slapped cold water on his cheeks and eyes, which helped the headache. In the mirror, his face looked prickly and older. He'd never gone this long without shaving. He rubbed his hands over the stiff blond bristles and imagined what a beard might look like. At least a beard would hide some of the shame that blistered the face staring at him.

They sat quietly at a small table. She had cooked everything he would have eaten at home—ham and eggs, hot biscuits, grits, even marmalade. At home, he would have been hungry. At home, kids would have been poking at each other and sloshing milk from their cereal onto the table, and a woman named Lizzie would be calmly wiping it up just as fast, asking him at the same time if he wanted another helping of eggs and his coffee warmed. At home, there would be ...

"A penny for your thoughts," she said.

He'd been staring at his empty plate and looked up at her looking at him over the rim of her cup. "Don't know they're worth that."

"Okay. Then a dollar."

He forced a bite of scrambled eggs and mumbled something nobody needed to hear.

"What?"

"Nothing. That'll cost you more than you got to give," which he knew was the wrong thing to say as soon as he said it.

"You don't know. I may have a lot to give." She said it with a smirk and a wink and the look on her face was sincere and terrifying.

Suddenly, a switch flipped in his brain, a right one for a change, he knew. "I gotta go," he said.

"What! You've barely touched your breakfast." She looked like she'd been slapped.

"I gotta go."

"Hap Pasley!"

"I gotta get my skinny little ass home." He stood up to move.

She was sitting across from him with her back to the door that led to the living room which was the way out. If he'd been a tad smarter, he'd have figured some way to be behind her, closer to the door.

She stood up. Her chair fell back and hit the floor like a shot. Her eyes lowered, half-lidded, like an animal before it pounces. "Now, Hap, honey. You don't need to go now. I've got some fun, fun, fun plans for today." It was the same low, husky voice she'd used when she grabbed his arm at the lounge, but her eyes were the same steely squint when she was talking about making her father pay. There was a door behind him but his keys and billfold were on the coffee table in the front room. He thought quickly for an excuse that would make sense.

"Gotta check on my kids. I'll be coming back this way tomorrow night."

"No, Hap Pasley. That's not it at all, is it? You just—"

"Really. I told my kids I'd pick them up at school. They're expecting me."

She picked up a spreading knife beside her plate and brought the flat side down hard on the tabletop. "You know something, Hap Pasley, I thought you were different." She began moving around the table toward him, the knife still in her hand, "but you're just like all the rest of them. Find 'em, fuck 'em and forget 'em. Isn't that right, Hap Pasley?"

She had it ass backwards but she was coming toward him, and he was too scared to argue with her. She moved closer, and he backed against a window. Then she stopped and glared at him, that look that was worse than hate, then slapped the knife again on the side of the table. He felt his whole body flinch. She was stiff to the point of trembling, and he saw the scream building in her. She was a woman gone mad, slamming and banging and shouting filth at him like he was some dog in a gutter. He was afraid to look up; he might see the knife coming down on his face. The way she was acting, she could have sliced him up with a spreading knife.

For a moment, silence. Then he heard running water. He looked up. She was at the sink, her back to him. He had a clear shot at the door. Pushing off from the wall behind him, he lunged for the doorway leading to the living room. His shoulder crashed against the door facing and spun him around, but he kept his balance and snatched the keys and billfold from the table. She was screaming again, and he knew she was right behind him. Her hands grabbed at his shirt, and it ripped as he made for the front door. Clutching the keys and billfold with his right hand, he fumbled with the bolt-action lock with his left. A sharp blow landed on his back between his shoulder blades then another lower down just above his waist. She was hitting him with knuckled fists as the lock finally clicked. He swung his right elbow back and felt it hit something solid and she fell back, giving him the split-second he needed to turn the door knob.

He swung the door open with her screaming "Sonofabitch! Sonofabitch! Sonofabitch!" at the top of her lungs, hitting him once more across his neck as he dove through the door and down the steps, scrambling on all fours into the snow. He didn't look back as he headed toward his truck which he never locked. He figured she'd come after him, but a passing car deterred her. He still didn't look back as he reached the truck and got in, locking the doors as fast as he could. When he finally looked, she was hopping up and down in the door with her fists clenched, like a wild monkey in a zoo cage, calling him names he'd never heard before. The motor turned slowly then started. He headed down the street without bothering to turn around. With the windows rolled up, he could still hear her when he turned the corner at the next block. He didn't know where he was and didn't care. Just being out of Maggie's place and alive was all that mattered.

The sky was bright and cloudless, and the snow melting some in the streets. He drove for several blocks, turned now and then, tried to find his way back to something that would give him bearings. The gas gauge needle was flat on empty.

Luck finally brought him to the intersection of a four-lane. The letters on the street sign said WINCHESTER. At the corner was a self-serve Texaco station. He turned in and stopped. His thoughts were whirling around and around, a few dropping into place to help him. He'd never know what would've happened had he not been able to get out of her apartment, except that somebody would probably be dead. He did know there was a woman back there who saw the face of her father in every man she met. The unfinished cigar in her kitchen came to mind, and he felt for the next poor guy who wandered into LuLu's looking for something to make him forget his hurt and loneliness.

He got out of the truck and walked to the gas station's restroom. It was locked. He had to go inside and ask for the key. A bald-headed skinny man behind the counter gave it to him. The light in the restroom was burned out, but he closed the door anyway and groped in the dark for the john lid which he finally found and pulled down, collapsed on it and cried.

13

Liz

The ground moved beneath her feet like the earth was drunk and gone mad and huge objects fell around her as she ran down a road that moved like a snake, almost screaming but too scared to scream, when she opened her eyes to Ruthie and Kevin bouncing on the bed beside her.

"Get up, Mommy. Get up."

"Yeah, Mommy. Get up."

"Time to eat breakfast."

"Grandmama says it's time for breakfast."

They looked cute mimicking each other, until they came together as if they'd been watching her dream. "Did Daddy call?"

She sat up and pretended not to hear. "Well, do tell. Aren't we bright and cheery-eyed this morning?"

"Did Daddy call?"

"Yeah. Did our daddy call?"

Their eyes begged as they spoke of him so personally, as if he belonged to no one else. Did her eyes show as much guilt as theirs did hope? Would they hear her nerves in her voice? She didn't want to bring them down.

"No, children. Your daddy didn't call."

Their little smiles dropped like pup tents when the poles are kicked.

"He could've at least called," said Ruthie.

"Yeah," said Kevin.

Conversation was scant at breakfast. Clinks and slurps and chewing. The sounds of eating were loud. Her mother made helpful statements to the children about school, that it would be a good day, that their teachers had neat things planned for them, that recess would be fun in the snow. They nodded with disinterest as she watched them slip further into worlds her thoughts couldn't reach, quiet worlds at the bottom of a glass or a bowl or a spoon, where strange shapes pulled on their imagination and gave rise to creatures and things never before seen. She'd leave them there in those worlds, as long as they came back. If they didn't, she'd know the problem was too serious and she needed to call mental health. This was what the books said, the ones on divorce she'd nervously checked out of the library, that when your children stop talking about their feelings, they were repressing, which wasn't good. She thought of what she might have repressed. But if something's repressed, you don't know it. Maybe that's what happened to her love for Hap. It just got repressed. She let her mind work that same row again, thinking there might be something else there to pick that would carry an answer. But it was too picked over and her bucket came up empty again.

She kissed the children and told them to be good and hurried them out the door. They tromped slowly through the melting snow toward the road, heads held down. Halfway, Ruthie turned and looked and waved. Then Kevin. They stared a while with blank faces then turned and continued toward the roadside. Her mother had called the bus driver and asked him to pick them up today until other arrangements could be made. Another reminder of one more thing she needed to do. The bus came slushing along and stopped, red lights blinking. They turned and waved again as the door opened, and she saw them disappear among the crowd of bobbing heads she remembered belonging to once. Though she couldn't see them, she kept waving until the bus was out of sight. An unnamable pain pushed against her eyes and spread down her throat. The sky was full of early morning sun, and she let it warm her face as she listened to the rain-like sound of the melting snow rolling from the roof, splashing along the graveled edge of the house behind the azaleas on which snowy patches still laid like shredded rags.

Her mother was washing breakfast dishes, and her father lay in his recliner watching The Today Show. Willard Scott was wearing another crazy hat and wishing happy birthday to people who'd made it to a hundred, and she was struggling to get to thirty. She walked down the hall to her room where whimpers were about to explode into a hunger cry. Her mother had bottle-fed Michael on milk she'd pumped from her breasts and left with her before leaving last night. He was probably clamoring for his own sweet place again. Like a little fighter, he buffed the air with his tiny fists then gobbled her up, slurping and gurgling on breasts that had needed the rest but were happy again to be there for him, to feel his need for her like that. Surrounded by her own childhood, she could rest and gather in the slack of something that had once felt so tight and strong, hopefully finding some sense and strength before facing her mother again, alone.

Soon, the familiar sound of granny shoes clomped down the hall. Her mother stood in the doorway for a moment before she closed the door behind her, turning the knob carefully so there was no click. She walked to the bed and sat down. As usual she wore no socks, and, as usual, her laces were untied. Her mother was not lazy. Bending over was just too painful.

"Hope you won't mind an old woman who just happens to be your mama prying just a little," she said, smiling faintly.

"No, Mama. That's okay."

"So. You went to check on Hap last night."

"Yessum." She fastened her eyes on the top of Michael's head, thankful to have something else to look at.

"Was he there?"

"No'me."

"Was the house all right?"

She couldn't lie but couldn't tell the truth either. She didn't know the truth, only that from the road in the dark something didn't look right. "Not really."

"What was wrong?"

"I don't want to go into it right now, Mama. Whatever might be wrong with the house is a trifle compared to everything else that's wrong in my life." She was immediately sorry she'd snapped, but this was going beyond a little prying.

Her mother blinked wide, like she'd felt a little sting, then leaned back and laced her fingers around a knee. "Well ..." She studied the ceiling as though reading something there. "I figure I could help, if somebody'd just tell me how."

How do you tell somebody how to help you when you can't tell them why you need help? Even if she told her about Billy Ray, which she'd never, that would only be telling part of the problem, the rest of it being a puzzle of a thousand pieces scattered and strewn over the past ten years, maybe further. How a marriage could stay together through fights and children and children growing up and leaving and boredom and old age till death, that was a far greater puzzle.

"Mama?"

"Yes, hon." Her mother no longer looked at the ceiling but straight at her, with eyes that seemed to read the question coming, as though they'd read it a long time and now braced for it.

"Do you love Daddy?"

"Of course. You know I do. What makes you ask a question like that?"

"I never see you hug or kiss anymore."

"Well ... we do," she stammered with embarrassment. "You just don't see it."

"Do you still, you know, do you still ... Mama, do you still make love to each other?"

In the long silence that followed, she watched the blood fill her mother's face and the smile she tried that finally came out, a little nervous laugh before she answered her. "For heaven sakes, child. Such a question. Why, of course we do. Such a question."

Seeing her mother squirm made her feel guilty, that she'd turned the tables and was the one doing the prying.

"I'm sorry, Mama. I just had to ask. I thought maybe there was—"

"Even if we didn't, wouldn't mean we don't still love each other. I'll swan. Don't see what that's got to do with things."

"I said I was sorry and—"

"Why, your dad and me'd never think of ... " Her mouth began to quiver and her hands fumbled with the buttons on her blouse. "Your dad and me'd never ... " She took a deep breath and closed her eyes to try again. "Your dad and me'd never think of leaving one another, no matter what." When she opened her eyes, the tears came, running in long streams down a face that was still trembling, struggling to stay strong.

She could only rock Michael as she watched her mother cry for the first time, surprised she wasn't crying with her. Maybe she was all cried out and the pain inside of her was dry but not dried up. It just needed time to gather and run again. What was coming out of her mother had been there a long time, coming out that way too, quietly, slowly, from some old pressure that simply couldn't break something as strong as her. Watching her mother cry for the first time was like being in a damp basement Sunday school room when she was a child and reading that Jesus wept. She didn't cry then either. Knowing that God could cry somehow made her feel bigger.

She let her mother cry in her quiet rocking way on the edge of the bed. Except for muffled voices on the television that sounded far off and the ticking squeaks of the rocker across the floor, the house was still as church before prayer.

Her mother finally sat up straight, wiped her eyes with the flat of her hands. The tears were still coming, but she could talk, seemed to need to.

"I'm sorry, hon. Don't know what happened to me."

"That's okay, Mama. I understand."

"Don't think you do." She wiped her eyes again and fumbled with her buttons again.

"What is there not to understand?" It was not a question she wanted to ask. It was just there and came out. When it did, her rocker came forward and stopped.

"There're just some things you kids've never known, I mean, 'bout your daddy and me." The tears had stopped, and she stared at the ceiling again. Her hands were in her lap rubbing on each other. "Understand now, we still love each other, and respect ... " Her voice bumped on the word respect then slipped around it, like a leaf will when it hits a snag in a river, "and respect each other. But there was a time ... " She paused and caught her breath. "This is hard for me to tell you, Lizzie, but now I think you need to know." She took another deep breath and steepled her fingers under her chin. "There were a couple of times ... "

Her mother's face was as serious as a death announcement. Whatever was coming next she knew she wasn't ready for, prayed it wouldn't be what she thought it was. She pulled Michael closer to her as a rush filled her face and her heart began to throb like it was beating for all three of them.

"You musn't hold it against your daddy. He was young and had a lot of growing up to do. The first time, you weren't even born. The second time, you and your brothers ... well, ya'll were young, and we protected you." She paused again, and her hands returned to her lap in a grip that could have crushed steel.

"Mama, what happened? Don't leave me hanging like this." She tried to calm her own breathing which was heaving her breasts so she feared Michael would lose his hold and start crying.

"He ... both times ... he saw another woman."

"Oh, Mama, don't tell me this. No."

"Yes, hon. You need to know. I believe you can handle it now."

"But I had no idea he—"

"Listen, Lizzie. It's over and done with. We both put it behind us."

She was feeling the shock as though a blade had been driven through her heart. Her father cheating on her mother. Her father, the man who led the evening devotions when they were growing up, who put them to bed with a prayer, who drove the family to church every Sunday and said no wrong and did no evil and worked the fields and came home tired and hungry each evening telling their mother what a great meal she'd cooked, popping her on the fanny sometimes when he said it and telling them all, day in and day out, what a great mama they had. Her father.

"How could you stay with him after that?" The question didn't turn on her until it was out of her mouth. An awful feeling spread through her, and she found herself looking at the old happiness in the family portrait on the dresser then at Michael's head again where his cheeks were working.

"It wasn't easy. Trust had to grow again. Not just with me either. He had to learn to trust hisself again which was prob'ly harder on him than it was on me."

The words hammered on her ears. She couldn't speak. It was as though her mind was being nailed down and couldn't move.

"Lizzie? You okay, hon?"

She heard but she couldn't answer. She wasn't okay. An emotion deeper than sadness and stronger than guilt was taking over, one she couldn't fight, couldn't hold off, and the tears she saw now were dropping onto Michael's fuzzy head and rolling down over his cheeks.

"Lizzie? What's wrong? I didn't mean to upset you, hon. I just thought it was time you knew, what with all you and Hap're going through, it might—"

"Don't worry, Mama. It's not you. It's me. I just need some time, to work through some things."

"And here I was coming in to help and just made matters worse."

"No, Mama. You didn't. I did need to know." She couldn't tell her how much. Nothing could measure that.

"Well, promise me you won't take it out on your daddy or think ill of him. Please."

"No. I won't think ill of him."

She glanced up and saw the grim look on her mother's face as she rose from the bed, moved toward her and patted the top of her hand before leaving. The sound of her footsteps going down the hall were slow and heavy, the laces flapping as though they were whipping something. Her mother would go to the kitchen where she would start lunch while her father faded in and out of talk and game shows on television. They might speak, and they might not. That no longer mattered. They didn't need to prove anything to anybody. For all she knew, and she could imagine it now, they had touched each other last night, stroked the same tired, wrinkled places, in the same memorized positions, the only ones they probably knew and would ever know, and said the same words that had kept them together all these years.

The room was emptier than before and lonelier, but that part was over. Her mother would never have to tell her again and would keep on loving her, just as she had her daddy. Her mother was big again, right up there with God.

14

Liz and Hap

The city was behind him as he headed east through open countryside, toward home. The sun glared overhead, and the land had a polished gleam that was almost too much to look at. In the distance, the highway shined like a new black leather belt laid out on a white blanket. A lone hawk sailed low across the sky, banked in the wind and lit in the top of a dead tree. Higher up a flurry of small birds flitted and twisted and dived like a school of kites in the hands of children. Fresh tiny tracks where dogs or rabbits or deer had run looked like tiny stitches connecting fence rows and flower gardens and tree lines. Some connected nothing, just meandered in crazy patterns in wide open spaces before disappearing into brush or down a creek bank or over a hill. Those he wondered the most about.

His back ached where Maggie had driven her blows, and he had to rub his neck from time to time. His leg still looked awful but felt better and no longer throbbed. At the service station he'd taken another of the pills Doc Boswell gave him and applied a touch of the salve. He was able to at least do that much for himself. Beyond that and filling up his truck, he didn't know much else he could do.

For anyone who'd been through what he'd been through, two hours was not a long time to figure out his next move in life. But it was all he had, which seemed unfair, that the rest of his life depended on what happened in his brain in the time it took to drive from Memphis to Hatchie. Would she even talk to him? He'd tagged her last. There was no telling what she had stored up for him. She might tell him to go to hell. Then again, maybe she'd had time to think and decided she couldn't just walk away from a ten-year investment that included the happiness of three children. He'd had time to think and had learned some things about himself, and her, if she'd just give him time to show herf. That was the thin thread of hope he clung to, that she'd give him time to work it all out, though he was still not sure what that might be. But time was on his side, if she'd just give him that, which was the only difference between him and the spider that bit him. The spider was dead.

He replayed the horrible nightmare with Maggie and saw her again, jumping and screaming in the doorway like a maniac. He wondered if she was still ranting and raving and banging and slamming around in her apartment. She was probably listening to some funky music, if she even did that. She didn't seem to be into cleaning up messes, just making them. With her life, she probably thrived on mess, wasn't happy unless she had one stirred up. After all, that was all she'd ever known and remembered. She was tied to her daddy like a bitch bulldog to a stake, growling and snapping at the world every time she hit the end of the chain, which in her case was a pretty damn short one. He cringed on that thought. His own wasn't very long either, but he didn't feel hate every time he hit the end of his, just hurt. He wondered how somebody could hate that long. You'd think it would eventually just die out. But Maggie probably needed hers. It probably got her up each morning, like it was her cup of coffee. He couldn't hate Lizzie. Not in ten, twenty, a hundred years. You can be mad and not hate. You can't hate somebody who's the mother of your children. He pressed harder on the gas pedal as his truck sucked up the long road home.

•　　•　　•

Except in a dream, she'd never been in an earthquake but imagined the aftershocks from the first jolt must come about as soon and as close together as what was moving through her. Miraculously, little Michael slept on her chest on top of it all, just above heart and lungs and nerves that were holding on. Between stretches of what her mother had just told her, she thought of Hap, where he was, what he was doing, if the sheriff's department could find him to deliver the papers and what he would do then, and how she would counter when he did. She wondered about her father, how she could face him knowing what she knew, wondering if he knew she knew, and what she'd say and if she could say it looking at him. And creeping in were images of Billy Ray and his one hundred acre tomb of memories and the big chunk of herself she almost threw away, kicking herself that she'd even considered something called happiness would be with someone like him in a place like that, wondered about that big piece of knowledge that somehow never got factored in. She rocked again and looked at Michael and felt at peace until they came again, the tremors, rolling through her mind just like that, aftershocks following a great upheaval in her world.

She didn't know how long he'd been there. Her father stood in the doorway. His head sagged pitifully to one side.

"Your mama said she told you."

"Yessir." She wanted to help him, but her thought bank was empty.

"I'm sorry, Sis."

"That's okay, Daddy." Strangely, she could forgive him.

"No, it ain't."

"That was a long time ago."

"Not when it hurts now. And it still does."

"If it didn't, you wouldn't be the daddy you are."

He blinked, and she watched his face, the struggle going on behind it. A tear hung for a moment in the corner of an eye then ran the slope of his cheek, around his mouth. She stopped the rocker and reached out a hand. He came toward her and stood by her, placed an arm around her shoulder and kissed her on the forehead. She felt his big body tremble and placed her hand on his and patted, letting her touch talk to him. Her mouth couldn't. He stayed a while longer, his arm still around her, then hugged her one more time, kissed Michael and left. Like her mother's, his steps down the hall were slow and sad. She said a prayer of thanks that she wouldn't have to carry a sadness like that with her into old age. Then one for him, that he wouldn't either anymore.

•   •   •

He felt he'd been gone a hundred years, but the town looked the same. The snow had melted in some places under a blue sky that looked like it might be around a while. Maybe he should call her. The thought spun around in his head like a dropped coin then clattered flat. No. That would just give her time to think. She didn't need time to think about what he had to say. What he had to say didn't require an answer that needed to be thought about. What he was going to say and do next came to him when he hit the city limits. Too much thinking had passed under the bridge to do it any other way, and his mind was tired from thinking.

He pulled into the One Stop to wash his face and buy some mints. His breath had to smell worse than a dog's. As he stepped from the truck, a sheriff's patrol car pulled beside him and Rooker got out. He swaggered around the front of the car and had some papers in his hand.

"Sure as hell hate to do it this way, Hap, but these here're for you. Millie at the Chancery Clerk's office called this morning or I'd 've told you yesterday." Rooker handed them to Hap like he was laying a rose on a casket before it was lowered.

Hap's heart and lungs knew what they were before his thinking did and he leaned against the truck to keep from sliding to the concrete. He said nothing and took the papers from Rooker and laid them on the seat of the truck.

Rooker walked back to the other side of the car and looked at him over the top of his sunglasses. "If I was you, Pasley, which I ain't you understand, I'd take them papers and kick a little ass," he said, then got in the car and drove off.

A transport rumbled through the intersection behind him. A car pulled under the awning for gas. Someone he knew.

He closed the door of the truck and hurriedly walked into the convenience store, on toward the back where he knew the restroom was, all the while wondering if his legs would make it. He closed the door and pulled the john lid down and sat and held himself until the shock leveled out and he could breathe normal again. He could still feel his heart, but not like it was going to beat him to smithereens. His father had died of a heart attack, and he'd always imagined how it would feel to go like that. He waited now just to see if he was going to live. Dying in a john at a one-stop was about as lonely as lonely could get, and he'd had his fill of one-stop johns. By God, if he was going to die, it would be with his family. He jumped up and leaned over the dingy sink and turned on the tap and splashed cold water over his face. In the cracked mirror, his face looked cut up, like death, but something inside told him he was going to live.

•   •   •

Probably from a need to stay busy, her mother had prepared more than her usual soup and sandwich lunch. She couldn't remember when she'd had a meal with just her parents. There had always been brothers and their wives and children, Hap and their kids, others. Now in the silence, with just the three of them, the kitchen seemed larger.

"You think he'll call?" her father said as he shredded a piece of roast with his fork and dipped it in a pool of gravy on his plate.

"I don't know," she said. "He's supposed to get the papers today."

Her mother sat quiet as a rock, which was different. She was usually the one talking and her father the one listening.

"That's pretty fast, ain't it, Sis?" he said.

She felt her neck straighten, but knew he meant no harm, that his own past was asking the question more than him. "Yessir. Guess my lawyer filed them the day after I talked to him." She didn't look up and kept her eyes busy on eating. Some things you couldn't hide from parents. They could guess she had planned everything, but they didn't need to know how long.

"What are you going to do?" he said without looking up.

"I guess I'll go to college and get me a degree."

"In what?"

"Nursing maybe."

"That so."

"Yessir."

"That's good. You're good at taking care of others. Guess you got that honest." He looked at her mother and smiled. She smiled back.

"A lot of it on her own, too," her mother said, breaking her silence. "Which may be part of the problem."

That was not a shot at her father, but she watched his head duck a little toward his plate like it was meant for him too. Somehow, it was something to smile at.

Her mother must have noticed it. "With Hap, that is," she added. Her mouth leaked a smirk.

The sound of a motor in the drive distracted them. The top of Hap's pickup sailed by the side window.

"Believe your first patient may be driving up now," her father said.

No one smiled.

•   •   •

He hadn't touched the neatly folded papers on the seat beside him, and wouldn't. He'd heard enough factory talk to know what they said. Lawyer bluff talk, lies, garbage. That would just make him mad. He didn't need to be mad when he talked to her, just firm with his back bowed. He'd thought of stopping by Joe Mack Freeman's office. Joe Mack was a country lawyer who helped poor folks, helped them so they'd come to him when they wanted to file a lawsuit, which was how he made a living. Ambulance chaser. Hap didn't need to talk to a lawyer to know she had no grounds. He knew that, too, from factory talk. His father could say what he wanted to about factories, but you could learn a lot listening to other people talk about their problems. He probably knew enough to serve as his own lawyer.

His first thought was to be formal and go to the front door and ring the doorbell. Hell no, he'd drive right around back and knock on the backdoor. He could just walk right in without announcing himself, like he always did, but he wouldn't do that. He'd be a gentleman, like Billy Ray Rather. That'd get her attention all right. He popped another mint in his mouth before he stopped.

•   •   •

She froze and grabbed a napkin as though it might hold a special strength. All along, she'd expected a phone call. He always called first to feel a problem out if he knew one was brewing. It wasn't like him to just show up at the doorstep of trouble. More like him to show up after it died down. Certainly not in the middle. Hap Pasley ran from trouble like a shadow from light.

She heard the truck door open and slam. Footsteps crunched on gravel then clapped on the concrete patio. She tried to catch thoughts as they blew past. Nothing stuck, nothing she could use anyway.

Through the storm door she could see him looking in. He could have walked in. He knocked anyway.

"I'll get it," her father said, scooting back his chair.

"No, Daddy. I'll talk to him. This is my problem, not y'alls."

"Just don't say anything you'll regret, hon," her mother said. "That's the only advice I got to give."

"Yessum, Mama. I won't."

She could tell his heart was pounding just by watching him eat for her approach, his legs shaking.

Her hand trembled on the latch as she opened the glass door. He looked like a stranger, like something dragged up from a hobo camp wanting a handout.

"Hello, Hap."

"Lizzie."

"You can come in if you like."

"I'd be real grateful if you'd come out here." He backed down the steps onto the patio to give her room. "Feel like we got some talking to do." He was clearly trying to keep his voice strong.

She hesitated a moment then stepped into the sunlight and down the steps. "You were supposed to go back to work today."

"I'm quiting."

"You're what?"

"There's not any noise out here. You heard it plain as daylight. I am quitting. Not going back."

Fire in his eyes was something new to her. "Hap Pasley."

"That's what they still call me in these parts. Still your last name too, I believe."

He was being sarcastic, but she felt sorry for him and wanted to be decent. "Like I said, you can come in if you like. Mama's got enough lunch if you want some."

"No thanks. Got something I wanna show you."

"What?"

"Can't tell you. Have to show you. Hop in." He nodded toward the truck.

She looked back through the glass storm door at her parents whose eyes were glued on them. "Where're you taking me?"

"I'll show you. Hope you know me well enough I won't harm you, if that's what concerns you."

Her first thought was to tell him no, that this was not a good time. But he was acting different, and she was curious. "I need to tell Mama and Daddy."

"You don't really need to, but I'll wait."

He was right, but it was for them, not her. She stuck her head in the door. "Everything's all right. He wants me to go somewhere with him. I'll be back shortly."

They said nothing, but the thin hope on their faces was unmistakable.

When she opened the passenger door, she saw the papers on the seat and pushed them aside.

He obviously noticed, but said nothing and started the engine, and they were off, in the same rattling contraption he'd dated her in.

She was surprised to find the old truck a comfortable place to be again. The feel of the springs and the bounce were the same. He drove like he always did, steering with his right hand, drumming the wheel with the fingers of his other, head turning from left to right, taking in everything but the road. But he'd never had a wreck. She figured he was fighting the same silence she was and decided to give them both some relief.

"Where were you last night?"

He thought a long moment before answering. "Memphis."

"Memphis?"

"Yes ma'am."

"By yourself?"

"Yep."

"You drove to Memphis by yourself, in this weather?"

"You know it."

"No I don't. You've never driven that far by yourself in your life."

He shrugged and faintly smiled. She was right. That fact had never occurred to him and jacked his confidence up a notch. "You're right. Guess there's a lot I've never done by myself that I'd better get used to." He turned in time to catch her eyes widen a little and her mouth tighten. "Idn't that what all this is about?" He let it go at that and turned his head the other direction and waited.

She couldn't name the feeling, but it was new and he was causing it. She'd heard of men going to the city and coming back different, but bad different, not better. "I'm not sure what it's about."

"You're the one that left."

She felt him pressing her too hard now and coming off cocky. "And I told you why."

"That dog won't hunt no more. Gotta come up with something better."

And coming back at her too fast for her to think. "I'm sorry."

"Me, too, though I'm not sure what for. Wish to God somebody'd tell me."

"I don't know what to say." That was the most honest thing she'd said in the past two days and it shut him up for a few seconds so she could think. She was dying to know where he'd been but that knife could cut both ways, so she aimed at his weak spot. Self-pity.

"How's your leg?"

"Now that you ask, it's better. Fact is, I'd almost forgotten about it." He pulled up his pants leg, not to show her but to let her see.

"Hap! It looks awful. You sure it was just a black widow?"

"Damn if that idn't what ever'body says," then he bit down on his lip.

"Everybody who?"

"Sheriff Cramden. Rooker. That's all. Just seemed like ever'body. My life hadn't been too full of folks here lately."

She watched his fingers drum faster on the wheel as they approached the main intersection. He put his hand out and turned left. The next few miles of bare asphalt were like a long wide pain passing through her. What she'd give to be able to repress the memory, not just of the last twenty-four hours but the foolish stream of fantasy that began on a spring afternoon on her porch when the man across the road stopped to see if her husband was in— and he wasn't. And they talked and talked and talked until it was almost time for her husband to be in, and he left only to return again and again when her husband wasn't in and she was caught up in a river and carried away too far to find her way to any shore, much less the one called home. Through the window, she kept her eyes on the passing familiar sights. Her hands toyed anxiously with a pink Barbie doll slipper she'd picked off the dash.

"I'll warn you before we get there," he said. "The place is in a mess."

The house came into view, and she saw the crumpled roof drooping on one side like the broken wing of a huge bird mired in the snow. She decided to say nothing and waited to hear the story he'd spin.

"I got drunk and tried to burn it down."

"Looks like you had something else in mind first."

"I did, but the chain saw quit on me."

She would've cheered him on had she been there. For once they stood on common ground with nothing to fight or argue about. She could've watched the place go up in smoke and invited the town to clap and sing.

•   •   •

Homer ran to meet them and barked along the side until they stopped. A handful of pictures he'd forgotten lay scattered in the yard. The bundle of clothes were still on the porch. If she asked, he'd tell her. But she didn't. She stood stock still looking at him, waiting for him to tell her what to do.

"Follow me," he said and walked toward a slight rise in the ground not far from the wood stack.

She obeyed, throwing a scare in him as she followed. "What happened to your shirt?"

He grabbed the first excuse that came to him. "Caught on a nail under the house."

"What were you doing under the house?"

"Looking for Homer. Now, you see that?" He pointed toward the river about a half mile away, where the long white slope from the hill ended in a line of trees.

"See what?"

"The river."

"I can't see it, but I know it's there."

Her arms were folded, and she was looking at him like he was crazy.

"That there's our future."

"Hap Pasley. Tell me the truth. Did you lay out in some dope joint in Memphis and the fumes haven'tt cleared your head yet?"

"No'me. Those fumes are dreams."

Then, with his arm still outstretched he swept it in a full circle. "We're going to bring that river to all this."

"Now I know you're on something."

"Government's paying me not to plant. Papers don't say nothing 'bout not breeding."

"Breeding? We can't raise cattle on this—"

"Catfish."

"Catfish?"

"Catfish."

"Catfish." She whispered the word with her head bent and her eyes amazed on the ground.

"I figured it all out. Came to me in a flash." Rooker was a far cry from a flash, but the Lord does work Himself in the most unusual ways, through the most unusual people. "One here. One there. Another over there." He kept drawing circles on the land with his finger. "Two behind the house near the woods. And over yonder," he pointed behind them "two, maybe three more."

"So. Eight or ten fish are going to feed us and clothe us and shelter us. I do declare, if you hadn't gone plumb nuts and think you're Jesus Himself on the Mount feeding the multitude. You've been snake bit instead of spider bit."

He considered briefly the unlikely possibility she and Rooker had formed a confederacy then realized he had to draw her a picture.

"You can rent a dozer for twenty-five dollars an hour. Would take a good man a week maybe, good weather permitting, to dig out eight or ten ponds on this property. A good pump don't cost that much. The county'd give us a permit to pipe water from the river. It'd create a few jobs and mean more taxes for them. Kids'd have a place to swim and fish. We could sit on the front porch each evening and watch our money break the top of the water. Shoot fire, folks up North eating catfish like it was the next best thing to sliced bread."

"Raise catfish?"

"You got it. Welcome to the Pasley Fish Farm." He scratched his head. "No. Better yet. The Pasley Fish Ranch. I like that better. Don't you? That's what farmers in the Delta are doing. Why hadn't somebody in North Mississippi thought of that. But they had. She was looking at him, eyes flashing, mouth grinning from ear to ear, even looking like a fisherman, three-day beard and all, smell, too.

"Hap Pasley. If you don't beat all."

She looked impressed, and he thought he almost saw her smile. He knew he was scoring points and was about to hit her with the big question, just like he'd planned, when they heard the sound and looked away from each other. A patrol car was working its way up the drive, bouncing up and down, slinging snow and mud behind it. As it got closer, he could tell it was Rooker. Why him again? He'd already given him the divorce papers.

Rooker sluiced up behind the truck and stopped and got out. His face was serious as he walked slowly toward them. He had a paper rolled in one hand.

"What can we do for you today, Mr. Rooker?" she said, trying to cover her nerves in politeness.

Hap looked at Lizzie, then at Rooker. "Rooker, you gave me the divorce papers. What is it now?"

Rooker stopped a few feet from them. His legs were spread and his thumbs hooked in his belt. "Lizzie, I gotta talk to Hap. Might be better if you stepped inside." His fingers on the hand not holding the paper were drumming away on his pants.

"I'd really rather stay right here, if that's all right with you, Mr. Rooker."

"What's going on Rooker? What's this all about?" Hap said.

"It ain't pleasant, Hap. Want you to understand I'm just doing my job."

"What the hell, Rooker? This don't make sense."

"Sure you won't go inside, Lizzie?"

"I'm sure, Mr. Rooker. I'm staying right here to find out what all this is about."

"Hap, Sheriff Cramden wanted to come with me and bring some backup, but I convinced him I could handle it by myself, that you wouldn't be a problem. Don't want you to let me down now."

"For God's sakes, Rooker. Spit it out."

"Well, I got a warrant here for your arrest and—"

"ARREST? You can't be ser—"

"Lizzie, sure would be better if you'd step inside for a minute," Rooker said.

"No, sir. Anything having to do with Hap, might have to do with me. I'm staying put."

"Have it your way then, but like I said, this ain't gonna be pleasant. Hap, some woman in Memphis filed charges this morning with the Memphis police. Now I ain't saying she's right, you understand, but she's claiming you raped her."

PART TWO

15

Hap

He rode up front with Rooker. Neither said a word. He was still too stunned and drained to talk, and Rooker seemed shaken as well. The handcuffs lay on the seat beside him. Rooker agreed not to use them if he came peaceably. But he didn't not until he screamed every cuss word he knew in front of his wife, who looked on dazed and helpless, and kicked the tires of his truck until his feet hurt and rammed the hood with his fists until they bled and heard Rooker read him his rights. That calmed him down, and he said he'd go peaceably, "to clear up this godawfuldamn mistake." He remembered saying that a lot, "godawfuldamn mistake." He was living a nightmare he never even dreamed he'd dream but was sure to now. Lizzie was somewhere behind in his truck. He'd given her the keys and told her to take care of it and the house and the kids, to be sure and tell them he loved them. She said nothing back, just looked at him with a childlike shocked face like he was a stranger who'd suddenly walked into her life—and was leaving just as quick.

He felt empty as a cracked shell before it shatters and falls apart. He saw his hands trembling first then noticed the wobbling of his knees, as if he couldn't feel them till his eyes saw them, the seeing causing the feeling. That was the sad state of his mind, that he had to see to feel, like feeling was something that couldn't run any longer on its own but was hooked up now only with his eyes. A pistol inestled in a holster beside the handcuffs. The strap was unbuttoned, and the gun looked to be loaded. If he thought he could get it out before Rooker caught him, he'd blow his brains out right there. The Lord never meant for any man to carry this much pain, not even Jesus. Jesus would have made it easy for everybody, too. The thought of praying was just that, a thought. He'd never done anything to deserve this. If this was what happened to God-fearing folks, hell was looking friendly. He did think about that a minute, a person carrying pain so long they no longer felt it, no longer felt anything for that matter, that hell might be like that, and if it was, he was getting close.

The silence around him was becoming worse than the emptiness inside, and he needed to talk, to see if he still could.

"Rooker?"

"Yep."

"What was the bitch's name?"

"Bevil. Remember that much. Think the first was Mary. Margaret. Something like that. Naw. Maggie. First name was Maggie."

"So that's it?" Hap said.

"What?"

"Her last name."

"And you didn't know hers? Damn, man. She sure 'nough knew about you. Your full name, model and make of your truck, described you to a tee. Even knew your life history. Ain't none of my business, you understand, but why was you fool enough to give her that, not to mention leaving your vest at her place?"

His hands slapped to his shirt. He hadn't even missed his vest. She must've taken it off him when she peeled off his shirt. The rub of the car seat against bare skin on his back reminded him of the rip in his shirt. He wanted to tell Rooker about that then caught himself. She probably told them she did it when he was supposed to be raping her.

"Report also says she ripped your shirt. I saw that back at your place. Tell you what, Hap. It don't look good."

"I didn't do it, Rooker."

"I ain't saying you did. I'm just saying it don't look good. I read you your rights, so be careful what you tell me."

"I didn't do it. I went to this topless bar, and she wanted me to go home with her. She seemed real nice. So, I went and when she had me three sheets in the wind, she jumped on top of me and proceeded to screw me like I was some kind of animal. Never seen anything like it. And that's the truth."

"I ain't saying it ain't. You just need to get yourself a good lawyer."

"Maybe you could stop by Joe Mack's before taking me to the jail."

"Nope. Gotta take you in first. You got a phone call coming to you. Call him from the jail. But, if it was me, which it ain't you understand, I'd call old man Fratello over there in Hickory Flat. Him and his boys the best criminal lawyers in the state. Maybe the whole damn South. That's what I'd do."

The Fratellos were good, and tough, rumored to be underhanded at times. But he figured they'd cost a fortune, and Joe Mack was a friend of the family's and wouldn't charge him as much, especially if he smelled a lawsuit in the air. "I'll call Joe Mack." He didn't thank Rooker for his advice. He was sick of him being right.

They approached the main intersection, and he scooted low in his seat.

"No offense, Hap." Rooker rubbed his nose and rolled the knot of tobacco in his cheek from one side to the other, then spat a brown blur into his Mason jar. "But you smell worse'n a three-day-old dead skunk."

He just looked at Rooker and slunk lower into the seat.

Joe Mack came right away. Hap hadn't seen the short, stocky lawyer in some time. Except for a small bald spot in the middle of his reddish-blonde hair, he looked his usual. Baggy pants.

Oversized sport coat, pockets bulging with candy mints and peanuts and keys that jingled when he walked. He was always cracking peanuts and sucking mints. His father had been a bootlegger, and town folks marveled when Joe Mack went to law school and passed. They marveled even more when he passed the bar and hung out his shingle and his father quit bootlegging. Hap had been with his own father to Joe Mack's office a couple of times, matters having to do with boundary disputes, legal titles and descriptions. The lobby of his office was always filled with folks who looked like they were on their last leg. He wondered how Joe Mack lived in a mansion and drove Jaguars and Mercedes with nothing but poor folks needing his services and his father no longer bootlegging. Then his father told him what an ambulance chaser was and about two separate million dollar lawsuits Joe Mack won. He didn't wonder anymore, except why he didn't dress better. He was glad to see Joe Mack, the first person that had anything encouraging to say to him in days.

"Don't worry, Hap. I've been involved in these cases before." He was sitting on the stool in the small cell like it was a personal perch. "The woman has to prove you raped her. That'll take some doing, with her being a topless go-go dancer and all. Jury'll be on your side, even a Memphis jury. They got lots of Baptists up there, too."

He was listening to Joe Mack's cocky confidence and remembered one rape trial that had the whole county talking. As it was told to him, Joe Mack had the woman on the stand holding a pencil in her hand. He was holding a long, thin tube big enough for the pencil to go in, but not much bigger. He told the woman to stick the pencil in the tube. Every time the woman jabbed, Joe Mack moved the tube. The woman never could get the pencil in the tube, and Joe Mack rested his case and won. Joe Mack was something else, but he needed more than a pencil act to get him out of this.

"But, Joe Mack, I got no witnesses, it'll be my word—"

"That's right. It'll be your word against hers. A pissing contest. But furthermore, and this is important, they got to extradite you first."

"Extra what?"

"Extradite. She says you raped her in Memphis. You reside in Mis'sippi. You can't even be tried unless the governor is willing to extradite you to Tennessee where you got to be tried. Now that may take some doing. Anybody in your family know the Governor or got connections with his office?"

He had to think. The governor was Boone Pepper, a businessman from the southern part of the state who switched to being a Republican and got elected on President Nixon's coattails. He knew that much from factory talk. He also knew from family talk that the governor was helped in Bedford County by Jake "Big Daddy" Rich. Big Daddy (everybody called him that because he was big, and like his name, rich) threw this big party every year called the "Chicken-Kicking Fling." Hundreds of folks'd come to his large farm for Bar-B-Q and beer and a cock fight or two. It was illegal as hell, but Big Daddy practically owned the sheriff, having financed his campaign, so nobody bothered the place. Last year, the state highway patrol got into the act because so many people were leaving drunk, which put a mild damper on things. His daddy and Big Daddy had been close friends.

"Yessir."

"And who might that be?"

"Big Daddy Rich."

"Good deal. You need to contact him, or I can. He owes me one."

"Meantime, I guess I stay cooped up," he looked around and lowered his voice, "in this place."

"Not necessarily. You could. Or you can make bond."

Bonds were all new to him, and Joe Mack went into the two kinds of bond, one where he had to come up with cash and the other called a property bond which had to be signed by two people in the county who owned property. He was thinking fast while Joe Mack talked. He didn't want to tell his mama. One of her sons being accused of rape would kill her. It didn't have to be fact or proven, just read and heard about, enough to tarnish the family name. She'd probably find out anyway, at church or from her sister or in the county paper. She'd probably sign, along with one of his brothers. The land he lived on was in her name alone, but he asked and Joe Mack told him the sheriff would probably go along with one of his brothers signing with her. The sheriff had to approve it all, Joe Mack said. All of this depended upon what the justice of the peace set bond at, he added.

"How much property y'all got out there?" Joe Mack said.

"All total, including Mama's, 'bout two hun'erd acres."

"How much on your place?"

"Thirty."

"What you reckon it's worth?"

"'Bout a hun'erd dollars a acre, which don't include what the timber's worth."

"So let's say two hundred dollars an acre. Judge'll probably set bail at around ten thousand. If you got a clean record, which you do, and he knows your family, which he does, he may knock it down to five thousand, which is what your place is worth. I'll have Sheriff Cramden or Rooker call a bondsman and get things rolling. Now, tell me what happened."

He went through the whole story, from start to finish. Joe Mack sat and listened, made a few notes from time to time on a yellow legal pad he balanced on his knee. When he finished, Joe Mack got up and said, "Don't you worry. This'll work out."

"'Don't worry? I was just trying to get back together with my wife, and all this comes up. It'll be in the papers, and my kids'll hear about it, and you tell me not to worry." He felt the tightness again in his throat and the settling in, like a lead weight in water, of a heavy sadness. "This is the worst thing that's ever happened to me, Joe Mack."

"I know Lizzie and her folks. I'll talk to 'em, tell 'em your side."

"Not about the drinking and screwing, for heaven's sakes."

"Well, I'll clean it up. Just don't you worry. You're not guilty, so don't act guilty. Don't look guilty either." He looked him up and down then thumped a finger on his shirt. "You need to take a bath and get cleaned up when you get out of here."

"What about my mama? This'll kill her."

"I'll talk to her, too. Right now I got to get over to the J.P.'s and get bond set."

Joe Mack rang on the bars with his class ring, and Rooker came and escorted him out. He wanted to call Joe Mack back and tell him how to handle his mama, but it was too late.

Rooker clomped back to the cell. "Gotta have your belt, Hap."

"My belt. What for?"

"Don't ask. Just give it to me. Regulations."

He unhooked his buckle and slipped his belt out and gave it to him. When Rooker left, he looked around the cell and suddenly knew why there weren't any sheets on the mattress, or anything else in that small concrete world that a man could kill himself with, except loneliness. A man could die, drown in that, with little help, loneliness and shame. He'd never committed a crime in his life, but just being where he was made him feel guilty as Judas. He started remembering every bad thing he'd ever done. Like a rope coiling around him, they began to squeeze him. He lay back on the bottom bunk and folded his hands across his chest and prayed for death.

16

Liz

She just stood and watched as he kicked and banged and cussed a blue streak that turned both her and the deputy's faces red. She still couldn't speak when he looked at her before getting into the car. Her mind felt like someplace flat and lonely where nothing grew, where bombs have been dropped from high up, the kind that don't whistle as they fall to let you know they're coming. Billy Ray. Herself. Her father. Now, her husband. Once she'd depended on all these, she thought, as she watched the patrol car wind its way down the drive toward the highway, until she could no longer stand to look in that direction and turned around.

The house. Two posts dangled where they'd been cut clean, as though sliced, and the left side of the porch roof seemed to hang, looking to fall any second. The screen door was busted, splintered across the middle and leaned outward, held only by a hinge at the bottom. Homer rubbed against her leg, and she reached down and patted him. She ran a hand through her hair then began picking up the pictures that were slightly sunken where the snow had melted around them. She placed them on the porch and checked the bundle of clothes. They were the children's, and they could use them. These and the pictures were all he'd intended to save. He did love his children.

She walked up the steps and placed the key into the lock, jiggling it until it finally turned and clicked. Homer was trying to follow, and she pushed him back with her foot. The smell of old smoke hit her, and she left the door open but closed the screen door, what was left of it, to keep Homer out.

Charred, black coals were everywhere. On the couch and chairs, the rug in the center of the floor. Smudges on the walls and ceiling marked where some must have hit. The windows were all down which was probably why the fire never caught. One by one, she opened them, to let out the smell more than to let in fresh air. Through one she saw them, the chainsaw and not far from it, a bottle, both half-sunk in the snow. He must have been bad drunk. He'd lied to her about why he was in jail and no telling what else. He could have at least told her he didn't do it before he left. That was probably the truth. Hap Pasley was childish and immature, but he wouldn't rape anybody, even drunk. There had to be a story behind it and she was sure she'd find out sooner or later. He probably had been with another woman. That did make her think again about him, re-look him. She didn't know he had that in him. She couldn't shake the thought that he was with another woman and wondered why the woman was mad at him. She couldn't shake that thought. It wouldn't have mattered the day before. She might've even welcomed the idea. Now, in a strange way, it mattered, that someone else felt the same about him.

A wasp buzzed against a window high up. Would it stay there and not bother her while she cleaned the house? She'd have been more likely to clean it if it hadn't been hers. She stopped and thought about that, why she was going to clean a house that twenty-four hours ago she'd hated and despised. Maybe she just needed to be busy.

She wiped away some coals and sat on the sofa. Her hands looked old as she rubbed them in the cold air. Quiet, as if a blast had gone off and made room for remembering ... *He and she away from the crowd, at last, alone. A small room and a large bed with a white spread that gave softly when they sat upon it. A tiny lamp on a small table and a yellow shade on the lamp and yellow light on the walls. The taste of champagne and the smell of his face, sweeter than the champagne and music somewhere, coming through the walls, and traffic hissing on the street below and a soft blue street light shining through the window and he kissed her and touched her gently and found her and the pain came that she wanted to come again, and when he brought it to her again it wasn't pain but something more than the opposite of pain and she didn't want him to quit, and he didn't, and they went on into the night like that, never sleeping until the yellow light on the wall was sunlight and the wonderful part of him was still in her and they fell asleep.*

17

Hap

He awoke to the sound of clanging metal. Rooker was opening his cell door.

"You can go now, Hap. Joe Mack got Judge Gaspard to set bond."

He swung his legs around and sat up. "How much?"

"Five thousand. Judge must've shown some mercy. Usually runs a lot higher for ... well ... for why you're here."

"I guess Joe Mack talked to my Ma—"

"We took the papers out to her, and she signed. She's pretty upset. Don't think I'd go 'round there for a while."

"Joe Mack didn't talk to her? He said he was going to talk to her."

"Guess he hadn't. She didn't know nothing about it."

"Oh, shit."

"She'll get over it. Women do."

"That's easy for you to say, Rooker. My wife's done left me, and now my mama'll disown me."

"Well, there's some good news. Sheriff helped you out, said your mama's signature was good enough for the property bond. Don't need another one. All you gotta do is pay the arrest fee."

"The what?"

"Arrest fee. State law. Ain't but seven bucks."

He rubbed his head and let out a groan. "All this is a bunch of shit, Rooker. One big bunch of shit."

"May be. But you got another problem. Well, I oughtta let your lawyer tell you 'bout that."

"Dammit all, Rooker. Out with it. If the shit's gonna hit me, let it hit me all at once."

"Naw, I'd better—"

"By dammit, Rooker."

"All right already." He was bent over and whispering. "We got others in here and don't want 'em to think you getting special treatment. The woman's got a doctor's report, or something like that, and it says she was sure enough screwed."

"Get Joe Mack on the phone. Now!"

"You get him yourself. I ain't the one screwed her. You the one been screwed for the screwing you done, if in fact you done it, you understand."

Hap shot out the cell door and headed down the dark hall that led to the front office where he'd used the telephone earlier. Joe Mack was out and would be the rest of the afternoon. He looked up his home number and tried it. No answer. He was about to walk out the door when another deputy he didn't know told him he had to pay the arrest fee before they could give him his things and let him go. His things? All they had was his belt. His checkbook was in his truck, which reminded him he didn't have wheels and he'd be stuck there until he could pay a fine and get his truck. He suddenly felt weak all over again and sat down in a chair beside the desk.

"Sorry 'bout all this, Hap," Rooker said. "If you'll just write an I.O.U. for the seven bucks, believe the sheriff'll honor it, knowing he knows you and your family and all. I'll be glad to run you back out to your house or take you to the Turpin's place to get your truck."

He resented Rooker's feeling sorry for him but needed it. The last thing he wanted to do was face Lizzie and her parents. He'd give gold to see his kids but didn't want them seeing him, at least not like he was. In the worst way, he needed a bath and clean clothes. All of a sudden, being friendly to Rooker became a necessity.

"Thanks, Rooker. That'll be a big help."

He scribbled off an I.O.U. on a small pad next to the phone and handed the note to the deputy who took it and placed it under a glass paper weight.

They were not yet out of the door of the jail, and he thought about his mother again. He'd meant to ask about her but Rooker side-tracked him with his wisecrack about women. He waited until they were in the car.

"How'd my mama take it?"

"Like I done told you, not good." Rooker hadn't cranked the car yet and was looking over the steering wheel with his head bent down like a man ducking something coming straight at him.

"What do you mean by that?"

"Just like I said, Hap. Not good." His voice was serious and he was still looking over the steering wheel as his key found the ignition and he cranked the car, like it was something he didn't need to see to do.

"That ain't telling me a whole hell of a lot, Rooker."

"Look, Pasley." He looked at him now, eyes squinting, lips pressed tight, using his last name which meant he was pissed, or about to be. "I'm trying to do you a favor, but you're turning into a real asshole, you know. All right, I'll tell you. She threw one of the wildest screaming fits I ever seen a person throw, old or young, male or female. She cussed me. She cussed Holder who went with me as a witness." Hap guessed Holder was the young deputy who took the I.O.U. "She cussed the sheriff. She cussed the government—"

"Did she—"

"You asked for this, Pasley, so lemme finish. Then she lit into you and didn't leave nothing left unsaid, and when she quit she was crying and shaking and saying it was the end of ever'thing and her face was so red I thought it was gonna burst right there. Then all of a sudden, she got real calm like, in a spooky sort of way, if you know what I mean. I mean the tears weren't even coming anymore, like a faucet'd been turned off, and she asked where she needed to sign. Hell, Holder's hand was shaking 'bout worse than hers in her fit when he laid the paper on the kitchen table. He stayed long enough for her to sign then left like he had ants in his pants. I stayed around a few minutes to make sure she was gonna be okay. It was weird. She wadn't looking at me, just staring a hole through me and said something 'bout that property never being good for nothing no way. When I left, she was still staring. Now that's what I meant by it wadn't good."

He'd asked for it, maybe even deserved it. He knew his mother would take it bad but not that bad.

The police band radio sputtered on and off with static. Rooker spat occasionally, and Hap could hear his own breathing through his nose. Those were the only sounds as they headed south out of town toward his place. His thoughts were loud, like a volume knob had been turned up. His mother and Lizzie. After his father's death, they were the only pillars that had kept his life propped up. Now, with them gone, he may as well have been dropped into a jungle in Africa. Between thoughts of them came bursts of anger toward Maggie, why she did what she did. His head was a place where two pistons hammered, one after the other. Hurt. Anger. Hurt. Anger. Hurt. Anger. When Rooker stopped the car, the hammering stopped too, and the dread of returning to the empty house overcame him. He managed something to say.

"Much obliged, Rooker. Sorry I was such a pain."

"Don't mention it. You gonna be okay?"

"Well, I'm not feeling much of anything right now. All my feelings been blowed away."

"If you hadn't've kept on and on—"

"It's not your fault, Rooker. I asked for it. Thanks for the lift. I do have one request."

"Will if I can."

"If you fellas do any patrolling 'round about out Mama's way, stop and check on her. I'd be much obliged."

"You got it. May call her first, though."

"Why's that?"

"She can't hear thunder in the back of that house. Met us at the front door with a shotgun aimed straight at us. Thought Holder was gonna draw."

He understood and got out and closed the door. Homer was right there jumping up on him. Rooker leaned over and rolled down the window.

"One more thing, Hap."

"Yeah. Make it quick. It's freezing out here."

"Do that dog a favor."

"Yeah?"

"Get a bath." He was trying to grin.

"Go to hell, Rooker." He forced a grin back at him.

He'd just cleared the top step when he noticed the screen door. It was straight, on both hinges, and someone had tacked the screen back in around the edges. The middle slat had been mended too. The door was locked, and Lizzie had the keys. The windows across the front were all up. He pulled the metal tabs loose at the bottom of a screen. It popped open, and he climbed in.

The house had been cleaned and straightened. Lizzie. She was the only one who could have done it. She had left the windows up to air it out, maybe even to give him a way to get in. He looked for a note on the kitchen counter, where she would have left one. There was none. He checked the bedroom and mantel. Nothing. Homer was scratching at the door. He let him in and watched as he lumbered to his usual spot on the rug in front of the fireplace and curled up.

He left the windows up but turned the heat on to cut the chill. As he walked down the hall to the children's room, he passed the gun case. The guns were gone. The glass was shattered, but the floor around it was clean. Lizzie wouldn't need the guns, so she must have taken them for another reason. She and Rooker or someone at the sheriff's department must have talked. No one knew it was Billy Ray he'd wanted to kill except Lizzie. She might have guessed it the way he showed his tail when she left.

He wasn't hungry but needed to eat something. He rummaged around in the pantry and found a can of Campbell's soup. It said ALPHABET on the label. After searching several cabinets, he located a pan in the one beside the sink. The instructions on the can were hard to find and even harder to read they were so small. The can opener was where he remembered, in the drawer to the right of the sink. His hands shook as he tried to fit the opener into place on top of the can. It finally caught, and he turned the butterfly-looking handle and watched the notches appear in the lid as the metal sheared cleanly from the rim of the can. He dumped the soup into the pan and added a can of water, like the instructions said, and placed the pan onto one of the coiled eyes on top of the stove. The letters under the knobs took more time to figure out. He studied them carefully then picked a knob with RF under it and turned it to "High" and stood back, watched as the coil under the pan turned from black to pink to orange then bright red. He'd gotten it right. The right knob goes with the right eye. She'd be proud if she could see. He'd seen bowls earlier but couldn't recall where. They were behind the second door he tried, neatly stacked. Maybe he was getting better at this. The spoons should be in the drawer beside the one that contained the opener, but it was filled with small towels and hot pads. He searched several more and found the spoons across the kitchen in a drawer beside the dish washer. Lizzie certainly had her own sense of order about things, he thought.

The soup lay flat in the pan, like a round peaceful orange pool. He watched, waiting for the first movement. Slowly, like the shape of the coil, thin yellow streaks swirled in the center. The edges began to hiss with tiny bubbles. Long moments later, large bubbles began to rise and pop. He stood back. Soon the soup was rolling and foam bubbling over the side of the pan. He looked around nervously for a lid. There was none, and he felt his heart start into a gallop then thought to turn down the knob. The bubbling and frothing stopped. The soup was quiet again. He could pour it into a bowl and eat. He had cooked something.

The first spoonful burned the tip of his tongue and scalded the back of his throat. Going down, the stream of liquid felt like a hot thread being pulled through him. A swallow of cold milk helped chase the pain, but the back of his throat kept burning like he remembered on mornings after nights of heavy drinking. Buttermilk was the only thing then that helped. He looked but found none in the refrigerator. He'd just have to eat slower and hope the raw burning stopped after a while. He blew on each spoonful, watching the tiny blond letters shiver and spin beneath his breath.

He made himself finish and rinsed the bowl and glass and spoon in the sink, guessing at where each went in the dishwasher. He thought of the things she would have done and wiped the counter with the green sponge that always sat on the side of the sink, next to the green frog that always held in its open mouth the rusty wad of steel wool which he used on the pan that didn't need it, putting the pan, too, in the dishwasher, guessing again. Doing the things she would have done made him feel close to her, closer than looking at pictures or remembering. It was like after his father died, he'd go to the barn and just be where he was, try to do the things he did—put on his gloves, sit on the same tractor seat he sat on, pitch hay with the same pitchfork he used, walk down bean rows, climb into the loft, kick the same loose board on the barn door. All that hurt more, but helped more, healed more, than anything else. But Lizzie wadn't dead. He'd have to see her again.

He tried to call Joe Mack once more. No answer at the two numbers he'd been given. He wanted to call his children but needed to feel better when he talked to them. They could pick up feelings on the phone better than if they were standing there looking at him. He wondered how children could do that, hear feelings better than grownups could see them.

He had closed the windows and the heat had been on, but a slight chill still hung in the air. The new roof and insulation wasn't working as well as he'd thought, but that was why he cut and stacked five cords of wood to last the winter. A fire would help the warming along, at least be something to look at and listen to. His mother was right about one being company. Both of hers were probably going full blast right now, feeding the one blazing inside her. Or maybe the other way around. He blinked his eyes. She stood in front of the fireplace like a wide-awake bad dream. He blinked again and shook his head and she was gone. He sure enough needed to build a fire.

Homer followed him outside. The fresh air did them both good, until he saw the chainsaw and bottle. He grabbed the bottle by the neck and threw it as hard as he could down the hill toward the highway. It thudded into a drift of snow. Homer didn't chase after it, just sat there at his feet looking up at him with wet stupid eyes. He left the chainsaw where it was.

He removed several layers of logs, down to where the wood was dry, and loaded his arms. Homer stayed as close to him as a small child as he tromped back to the house. It was as though both knew they needed the other, for more than just company.

The logs caught quickly from the kindling and were soon crackling and whistling and spitting wild sparks, sending roaring flames climbing the sooted flue. He undressed in front of the fire, standing so close the heat almost burned. One by one, he tossed each piece of clothing into the flames. First his socks and blue jeans. He waited for those to burn, watched as the smoke curled white around them before they caught in the flames and burned to black flakes that floated up with the sparks. Next he threw his undershirt. Then his undershorts, which he ripped. Last his shirt, which he ripped, too, again and again, feeding the rags to the fire as one might feed a starving beast. Homer began barking. First at the fire then at him standing there in front of it butt naked.

The bathroom was spotless and had that piney smell, the one it always had after Lizzie cleaned it. Why'd she do that? Not just patch up the screen door and sweep up his mess, but clean their bathroom. Matching towels and bath cloths were neatly folded across the racks around the tub. A new bar of Ivory was in the soap dish on the corner of the tub, like company was coming. Next to it was his old Gillette safety razor, the one she shaved her legs with. Did she leave it or forget it? One toothbrush hung in the holder beside the cabinet mirror over the sink, a reminder.

He turned on the hot wate over the tub, tested it with his hand, adjusted the cold faucet, let the water get as hot as he could stand it before stopping the drain. He wouldn't wait for the tub to fill, like he normally did. The water burned his feet at first but just for a moment. He watched them turn pink. A splash hit the wound above his ankle, a sharp little sting that went away quickly. He bent over and examined the spot. It looked about as bad as Doc Boswell said it would and everybody said it did, but the soreness seemed to be going down. He touched it to make sure. The water would help it, even if it stung. His grandmother always told him that meant healing was going on, when the medicine smarted. If that were only true about hurts of the heart. Sitting down was like easing into a friendly fire that warmed and soothed about as quickly as it burned. He flinched as he entered and then prepared himself for the icy shock when he leaned against the back of the tub, which was just that, a shock that, too, was soon gone. When your insides are in a mess, some things on the outside are like that, make you feel good even after they hurt a little.

As the water plunged into the tub, he closed his eyes and felt the heat slip in around him, remembering as a child the warm soothing feeling, water creeping around his toes, over his arms and legs, his privates, covering his stomach. He'd slide down to feel the warm again around his neck, up to his chin then go all the way under.

He was twelve when he was baptized, in the church that was sure now not to vote him a deacon. The water was not warm but cold. The preacher was a big man with white hair and white bushy eyebrows and a large red nose, the last thing he remembered seeing before closing his eyes and leaning back. It was almost like going under in his bathtub at home except someone was there holding him and wiping his face with a towel when he came up and said a prayer about his being saved, that all his sins were washed away, in the name of the Father and the Son and the Holy Ghost. He wished to be there again, starting over, all his sins washed away. Somebody lied to him.

He turned off the faucets with his toes and let the quiet set in. The bar of Ivory smelled strong and felt slippery in his hands. It slid across his skin as he guided it into every crease and wrinkle of his body, every nook and cranny, rubbing again and again, scouring his crotch and penis over and over, rubbing until his skin became squeaky and red as sunburn.

He returned the soap to the dish, and his hand touched the razor. He picked it up and turned it in his fingers. With a single twist, the top opened and the blade lay blue and flat with silver edges. He carefully lifted the blade from the razor and placed the razor back on the edge of the tub. He held the blade up in the dim light from the single bulb over the sink, wishing it were out. He'd only heard stories and seen movies. They said it only hurt when the blade nicked the skin, that the rest was painless. His thumb traced an edge then lifted a wrist to the light, where he could see the thin blue trails of veins. All he could think was painless, making the inside feel as good as the outside.

18

Liz

The snow was melting along the edges of the highway and running in small streams as though there had just been a rain, but the sky was clear, not a cloud in sight. More birds sat on the utility wires. They looked like strings of commas on lines where nothing was written, or could be. Occasionally, one would drop down along the fence rows for a morsel then fly away. Her children would be there when she arrived, and she had nothing for them. They would ask about their father, and this time she would lie to them.

Tomorrow, that clear splendid dream, that had given her hope and pulled her through each day, was gone. Not even pieces of it left, nothing to cling to. Why was she leaving now? Where was she going? She could live with her parents. But how long? Till what? Or who? What was she running from? Toward? Why? Questions, one right after the other. No answers. Just questions, as many as the telephone poles she passed. Crosses, she thought. They look like crosses. Jesus died on a cross on a hill. Jesus was not a question. He was an answer. She passed her church and thought about Brother Hammingtree. She could stop and talk to him. Maybe he could help. Maybe he had some answers. His face had looked kind when she told him. He had shaken her hand and looked understanding. She didn't have to tell him about Billy Ray. That was over and done with. The horrible memory moved inside of her like a worm, eating her up.

She couldn't stop at the church. She drove on.

The children clambered out the backdoor of the house as she stopped the truck. Their faces were bright and smiling, as she'd expected they would be.

"Where's daddy?"

"Where's daddy?"

"He's tending to some business," she said, feeling the tightness in her face as she tried to smile with them.

"When's he coming?" Kevin said.

"I'm not sure. His business may take a while."

"How much of a while?" Ruthie said.

"A long while. How was school today?"

"Fine," they both said.

"Just fine?"

"Yes ma'am," they both said again, together. She saw there in their faces what she felt in hers, an uncertain courage, struggling. Theirs seemed stronger.

"Well, get your coats and gloves and caps on. You can play a while in the snow."

They scampered inside and came sailing back through the storm door before she could open it.

Her parents were sitting at the table as though they'd never left. Their faces were grim, almost sad. She told them the news, and they listened quietly, with looks of disbelief. When she finished, they made a few comments. That it couldn't be true, that there must be some mistake. Whatever Hap was, he was not a rapist.

"I agree," she said. "Whatever happened, I can't help but feel it'll all get worked out. I've just been concerned about the children. They mustn't know."

"No. They mustn't," her father said. "They mustn't know ... any of this." He hesitated on the last words, like they were too big for him to say.

Her mother nodded in agreement.

She got up to leave the table, and her mother touched her hand. "Lizzie. A man called while you were gone. He wouldn't leave his name. He just said you'd know what it was about and asked you to call him."

She froze and looked through the storm door at the children tumbling in the snow.

19

Hap

It stung like a paper cut. There was a little squirt of blood then it ran in a steady stream down his arm into the water. His heart thudded in his ears, but he saw it beating through his wrists, tiny bumps of blood coming out with each thud, the bumps quickly joining the stream. He switched the blade to the other hand and made the same quick swipe on his opposite wrist then put the dripping blade on the ledge of the tub and watched as the thick red streams bled into the water on both sides of him, coloring the water like a slow leakage of dye, drifting downward, swirling into his hairy crotch and around his limp penis, like that was where it needed to go first.

He leaned his head back and closed his eyes. His mind was doing it, too, bleeding memories from the far edge of his childhood: ... *his hand pinching in the swing chain, looking at the rust in his palm thinking it was blood, crying, mama wiping it and kissing it, daddy yelling at her quit that, woman, quit it, you'll make him a sissy, he needs to learn to hurt, he needs to learn to hurt, and granddaddy yelling at daddy telling him to quit yelling at mama but she keeps on wiping and kissing, telling him it'll be okay, it'll be okay but it wadn't okay for billy ray to hit him in the nose on the way to school, running, crying all the way, blood all over his white shirt, cain't tell the teacher why just cain't mama taking him back to school to tell miss thompson telling her when i wouldn't, mama calling billy rays house mama telling billy ray too the next day what would happen if he did it to her little Hap again mama doing it all daddy raising hell when he came in from the fields and heard it mama lying beside me her arm across him sleep coming on eyes leaving the road a second only a second the car crashing off the pole hitting another car sleep coming on fast people yelling blood in my mouth something hard like bits of hard candy there too teeth broken coming out in my hand sleep coming daddy waiting with the strap mama standing between thems arms around him sleep coming yelling at daddy don't you dare don't dare sleep sleep don't don't sleep don't sleep don't die don't sleep don't die and leave your children without a daddy the worst sin they need a daddy don't die the worst sin don't kill ...*

He opened his eyes, the walls curving bright and fast around him like sunlight moving and the water a dark red flood carrying him away, and he wanted the moving to stop, and it wouldn't, and it seemed there was nothing to hold on to, that he was floating away. He found the cold sides of the tub with his hands and pushed up hard. His body rose slowly. He leaned across the side and pushed himself over with his feet, bloody water sloshing onto the white tile, red streams running everywhere across the floor that was spinning with the only thought in his head. Stop the bleeding. Got to stop the bleeding. He tried to stand up and couldn't. He reached for a towel and pulled it from a rack and started dabbing at the cuts, but the blood kept coming. Bandages? Tape? Somewhere in here. Lizzie kept them in a bathroom cabinet. He tried one. Then another. Just bottles. The smell of her hair and face and hands. Can't die. Children. Got to stop the bleeding. God help me. He opened the cabinet under the sink and saw the first aid kit. The can of bandages fumbled in his hands and dropped onto the floor popping open the lid. His eyes weren't focusing good. He picked up a bandage and opened it. His hands were trembling, and he couldn't get the plastic off the adhesive part and threw it on the water-soaked floor. He saw the wide roll of tape and grabbed it. There was a flap, and he took it in his teeth and pulled, then managed to hold the roll with one hand while he ripped a piece off with his teeth. He knew to pull tight when he got it on the cut, to stop the flow. He was able to rip another piece and slap it on his other wrist, almost missing the slice where the blood was oozing out. He had no idea how much blood he'd lost and was afraid to look in the tub. His head was swimming, and he was too dizzy and weak to try standing up again, so he stayed on his hands and knees and crawled. The bedroom was next to the bathroom. If he could get there, he could get something around him and use the phone. He felt feverish and weaker than when he had the flu but something was moving him on, maybe God, maybe his kids, maybe both. Homer turned the corner from the den and slunk back then let out a low moan and came over and licked the side of his face. He talked to him and told him to stay close like he was a human who could help then thought a human can do a lot when living's just the other side of dying. He turned into the doorway to the bedroom and stoppe to catch his breath. He finally made it to the bed and pulled himself up and rolled over. Homer laid his head on the edge and looked at him with big glassy eyes that seemed to know what was going on but couldn't help. The phone was near his head on the nightstand. He was able to reach it by turning sideways. The numbers ran together, but he guessed where the zero was at the bottom and punched.

"Operator," the voice said.

"Operator … " He had to stop and get his breath again.

"Yes, this is the operator."

"Operator, I need help. Get me some help. My name is … I'm Hap … Pasley … I'm at … "

"Is this an emergency, sir? I've got your number. Is this an emergency?"

"Yes … yes … "

"Do you need an ambulance?"

An ambulance. Not an ambulance. He didn't want an ambulance. But, "Yes … I think so … hurry."

"Yessir. Stay calm. I'll contact emergency services in your … "

He didn't hear the rest. The phone dropped from his hand, and he lay back on the bed. The ceiling dimmed then faded.

20

Liz

She went to her room without saying a word to her parents. Michael was asleep in the baby bed. He would need to feed when he woke up. She rocked to pass the time, time she needed to think of an excuse to leave the house. The last thing she needed was Billy Ray calling her here. No. The last thing she needed was talking to him again. Period. She had nothing to say, nothing. She had only herself to talk to in the awful silence broken only by the measured clicks of the rocker across the floor and Michael's soft gurgling snores and herself was not talking back.

She fed Michael, and he went back to sleep. She returned him to the baby bed then waited for her mother to call the children in from playing, to wash up before supper. She walked quickly through the den and gave the best excuse she could think of, flimsy as it was. Her parents would see straight through it but wouldn't say anything in front of the children.

"The truck's about on empty, and I'm going to get it filled up before dark and take it to Hap. He might need it. Mind your grandma, kids. Get your bath when you finish your supper. I'll eat when I get back. Won't be gone that long." She kept talking all the way out the door but felt her parents' eyes on her.

The sun was alone and low on the sky, a clear orange sight that bathed the melting land and rooftops and trees with a copper glow. The streetlights were coming on as she entered the Hatchie city limits. The One Stop was busy, but it was the only decent place she could think of that had a pay phone. It was no easier on a Monday than on a Sunday night calling a man who isn't your husband from a pay phone. At least it was daylight, barely. Night was moving in quickly over the low hills to the east.

He picked up on the first ring.

"Hello," she said.

"Lizzie? My God I've needed to talk to you. I'm sorry for calling you at your—"

"Billy Ray. I can't believe you called my parents. That's the last thing they needed—"

"I'm sorry. I didn't know what else to do. I was going crazy not being able to at least talk to you, to tell you how sorry I am about last night."

"No need to. It's over and done with. We were both wrong. I'm sure we're both sorry."

"Over and done with. Just what happened you mean. Just the—"

"Wait a minute, Billy Ray, I can't hear you. Wait a minute."

"I'm talking as loud and plain as I can."

"There's a siren. An ambulance is coming down the highway. Wait a second till it passes."

She turned her head to see the red lights flashing as the orange-striped vehicle flew through the intersection where cars had stopped and pulled over to let it pass. She covered her ear to muffle the high shrill of the siren, watched as the flashing lights continued south toward New Albany and the nearest hospital. She wondered for a moment who it might be, then turned her attention back to the phone.

"Now I can hear you. Go on."

"You don't mean we're over and done with. Just what happened. That's over. It won't happen again. I promise."

"No. We're not over. We were never started. The Lord knows that, and both of us should be on our knees asking for forgiveness."

"You're not saying what I'm hearing. Please say you don't mean it."

"Believe me. I mean it." The words just came, strong and clear. She didn't believe it herself, that she was actually telling him it was over.

He began to cry. First in low jerky sobs then bawling into the receiver. "I can't believe you're doing this to us. Not even giving us a chance. I lost control. I admit that. I'm sorry for that. But you're the only thing in my life. I need you. I love you, Lizzie Pasley. You must believe that. You must. You must."

They're all such pathetic creatures, she thought. Men. Do they love you because they need you or need you because they love you? She wanted to believe the latter, but knew it was the other. Without women, they were lost little boys, crying in a lonely world. Hap was not the only one. No matter how rough and tough they looked and seemed and behaved on the outside, down deep on the inside, they were just lost little boys needing another mama. That's why mamas were strong and always there. But she didn't want to be any man's mama . . . or whore. She'd had enough of one and come close enough to the other to suit her soul.

"I believe you love me." A man walked toward her to get into a car parked beside the truck. She waited until he was inside and the door slammed. She moved her mouth closer to the receiver. "In your own way, I believe you love me. I believe Hap loves me. I just don't know why I'm loved, much less who I love. I do know I can't be seeing a man and still be married to another. I can't do that to my children. I can't do that to my parents. To myself. Or to God. And that's that."

He was whimpering now into the phone, like that was all he could do or say, like his crying was winding down and he was finally hearing her, finally accepting the hurt.

She needed to help him along, slam the door shut. "Billy Ray." She looked around to see if anyone was watching or listening. "Never call me again. Never again. At my parents. At my home. Never. Do you hear me?"

"Yes," he said, sniveling. "Yes, I hear you," in a stronger tone. "I think I hear you loud and clear."

"I don't think there's anything else we have to say to each other." She said.

"I just don't believe this is happening. I just don't believe—"

"Believe it, Billy Ray," she said, forcing strength into her voice. "I can't love a man, much less marry one, who's committing adultery with his land every day and just needs a woman around to make all the pieces fit. And you barely needed that, much as I could tell." She was saying more than she meant to and needed to find a way to hang up.

"What do you mean, barely needed that?"

"You know what I mean. Just like most men, you only needed me for one thing." In her mind, she glimpsed Hap walking toward her from the stacked wood, the expression on his face and what happened to it. "Almost most. I've got to go Billy Ray. The children are waiting supper for me. I just had to call and tell you not to call me there again, ever. I'll call you if and when I need to. Goodbye," and she hung up.

She put another quarter in the slot and dialed. A busy signal. She tried once more, thinking she could have misdialed. Busy. Someone had to be there if the line was busy. She could try again later from her parents'. That way the children could even talk to him.

As she walked back to the truck, she heard the sound of the siren again, in the distance, leaving from wherever it had stopped, fading south. Hearing a siren always touched her. It meant someone was hurting, a reminder of how suddenly sorrow can come into the world. She hoped whoever it was would be all right, that they wouldn't die.

She was about to open the door when, breaking through the cold air, she heard another siren, coming again from the north. The steady shrill switched to whoops and she watched as the red and white flashes whipped through the intersection and the whoops switched back to siren. This ambulance was going faster than the first, she thought. She could still hear the siren as she drove home. It stopped for a while then started again. There must have been a big wreck somewhere south of town. Two ambulances meant something awful. She drove on in the last light hovering over the low hills, thankful her family was safe at home then remembered. She'd forgotten all about filling the truck up.

She could hear the children crying before she opened the back door. Ruthie was curled up in her father's lap on the recliner. Her mother held Kevin on the couch. Both were sobbing. The faces of her parents were pale, their eyes jarred, like they'd seen something horrible and the damage was piled up behind them.

"What happened?" she said. "What in the world's going on?"

"The phone rang while you were gone," her mother said. "Kevin got to it before your daddy or I could. Of course, we had no idea."

The children cried louder. She walked over and patted one then the other. "Well, go on."

Her mother continued. "We just thought it was someone asking for you, then Kevin got all excited and starting asking questions. He started crying, and Eulice got the phone. It was a deputy from the sheriff's department. Anyway, Hap had to be rushed to the hospital."

The children burst into bawls.

"Oh no," she said, holding a hand over her heart where she felt it hammering.

"We had to tell the children," her father said. "Kevin already knew something, and we thought it was best."

"What happened?" she said.

"We don't know," her mother said.

"Which hospital?"

"New Albany. The ambulance had to come from Walnut," her father said.

"I saw it go through town. But there were two of them, about five minutes apart. I thought it must've been a wreck."

"I wanna see my daddy," the children were crying, over and over.

The phone rang.

Lizzie moved quickly to answer it. It was Mr. Rooker. He was choking on his words and almost crying. She wasn't able to let him finish. "Oh my God, no. No. Oh, my God." The phone fell from her hands, and she covered her face.

21

Hap

He felt his toes wiggling then the cold before he heard the tingling and clinking sounds and far away voices that seemed to run together. He tried to open his eyes, but a bright light shut them and burned on through his lids. A hand held his right arm. He felt a sharp sting and the hand let go. He tried to move his arm, but something held it down. He could move his head from side to side, but the bright light was there too. Through his nose came a smell he couldn't name.

Cold. Everything was cold. And dry. His throat was dry. He needed a drink of water and tried to see if he could talk.

"Water. A drink of water. Can someone . . . give me . . . a drink of water?"

"We'll give you some in just a minute," a woman's voice said. It sounded nearby and was soft and warm, something he wanted to touch.

"Where . . . am I?"

"You're in a hospital. You're going to be okay."

He was about to ask why then remembered. Bathtub . . . water . . . razor . . . blood . . . stupid . . . what he did was stupid . . . his children . . .

"Try to be as still as you can, Mr. Pasley," she said.

"What hospital . . . where?"

"New Albany. Now try to be quiet and rest," she said, an edge in her voice replacing the softness.

He quit trying to open his eyes or catch thoughts that wouldn't stay still. A sheet of yellow glare lay over his eyes. For a long time, the voices came and went, along with the sounds. The woman's voice. He wanted to hear her again, wondered if she'd left him, if he was alone again. He felt movement. A shadow passed over the yellow glare, like a cloud passing over the sun, and he could open his eyes. Long fluorescent bulbs slid over him, huge ice trays of frozen light floating overhead. A piece of ice. What he'd give to have a piece of ice in his mouth. White shiny walls moved along both sides. He was being pushed down a cold, dry hall.

"Where am I going?"

"I'm taking you to your room." Her voice again. "So you can rest and get your strength."

He strained his head against his neck and rolled his eyes back. A long red tube ran up to a small red bag that hung on a hook just above him.

"What's that?"

"You lost a lot of blood. We're just putting it back."

He strained further and could see her red lips, smiling, and blonde hair swinging against her cheeks. His neck ached, and he had to bring his head forward. A face flashed before him, and his body jerked, but he couldn't move. He could see his arm strapped and the long tube ending just below his elbow. The face flashed again.

"Be still, Mr. Pasley. You might yank the needle out of your arm," she said.

"What's your name?"

"Margie."

He felt his mind flinch along with his body when she said the name. "You have a daddy?" Like a knee jerk, the words coming out, too late for the realization he'd heard it wrong, that she'd said "Margie" and not "Maggie."

"Yes, I do. But, Mr. Pasley, you really need to be quiet."

"You're a nurse?"

"Yes."

"You'll be taking care of me?"

"Yes. At least until eleven. My shift ends then, but you be quiet. You need to save your strength. Try not to talk."

Not talk? She didn't understand. He needed to talk to somebody. He needed to explain.

"Does my family . . . has my family been told?"

"No one's been contacted yet. We were waiting for you to come to and feel better. There was no identification on you."

His billfold. Still in the truck. He remembered that.

"All we had was your name. We analyzed a sample of your blood to get your type."

No one knew yet.

A voice came over the loudspeaker. "Code Blue. Code Blue. Code Blue. ER. ER. Code Blue in ER."

People were rushing by, going in the opposite direction.

"What's that?" he said.

"Just a message for doctors and nurses. It doesn't concern us. I'll have you to your room in just a minute."

They turned a corner. The message came over the speaker again. The nurse pushing him spoke to someone coming out of a room, a man dressed in white, and asked if he could help her get Hap into his room and into his bed.

A room. God please, yes. Just get him to a room and close the door and put up a sign saying no admittance. Then come back. Let the nurse come back and just talk to him. He wouldn't say anything, he promised, as long as she'd just keep talking to him, telling him he was going to be okay. Not just him. But his life.

They turned again and entered a dark room. The man turned on a light and walked to the other side of the bed. He looked young and had a beard. The man's arms went under Hap and he felt himself lifted up and laid onto the bed. He was sitting up and could see the nurse clearly now, her face like an angel's, small and round and framed by hair that hooked under her chin. She smiled at the man as he left and thanked him. His name was Michael.

"Are you all right?" she said.

"Yes," he lied.

She held his wrist and looked at her watch then wrote something on a small clipboard and turned to go.

"Please stay," he said. "Don't leave."

She smiled again. "I'll be right back. You just rest. Do you want me to let your head down more?" Her eyes were the only color he could see, blue as heaven.

"No. I'm okay. I just don't want to be alone."

"Don't worry. You'll be running me out before the night's over." She got to the door and stopped and turned. "Do you want me to call someone for you?"

Lizzie. He needed her more than ever. But she was gone. This would do it for sure. Besides, he wouldn't be able to face her if she did come. She wouldn't feel sorry for him. She'd despise him. His children. He'd let them down. Good daddies don't do this, they don't cop out on their kids. His mother. This would kill her for sure. "No. Not yet. I need to think."

"You need to rest. Then think. In that order. I'll be right back."

"I could use a drink of water."

"Thanks for reminding me. I'll bring you a pitcher full. How's that?"

He nodded and tried a smile. "With ice."

"The television button's right there at your side," she said. "Turn it on if you like, if that will help. Monday night football comes on after a while, if you like football."

He didn't. She left and a heavy wave seemed to sweep down upon him from the dark corners, the dark television screen boring into him like a huge eye and the dim blank walls the color of skin and the darkness stretched beyond the windows into the night. He didn't think it possible, that a person could feel and hurt any worse. More pain was ahead, but he wouldn't go back. Maybe what he'd gone through was meant to be. If baptism could be like this then more folks would believe, really believe, and get their acts together. He'd have to die sometime, but not before living to see his sons hit their first baseball, catch their first fish, kill their first deer; living to watch his daughter play her first song at her first recital, dress up for her first date, cheer at her first ballgame; living to see them walk proudly and get their first diploma: living to give his daughter away and stand by his sons on their wedding day, living to hold their first children. Living. They wouldn't stop, the firsts he wanted to live to see and feel and hold, stacking up in his mind like clouds on a summer afternoon. He tried to hold his eyes open. If he closed them, the tears he could feel gathered there would run, and she'd see them if she walked back in. Images swam on the screen above him. Ruthie and Kevin and Michael, fading in and out, smiling at him, calling to him with silent lips he knew were saying Daddy, Daddy, Daddy. Even little Michael's mouth moving like that word, Daddy... Then they were gone. He couldn't keep them open any longer, and his eyes closed.

He didn't know how long he'd been asleep when he felt the warm hand on his wrist. She was back, looking at her watch, checking his pulse again. Her smile was gone, and she seemed in a hurry, or nervous, he couldn't tell which.

"Is it okay?" he said.

She didn't look at him or talk, just nodded. Maybe they don't tell you anything because it might upset you.

She began placing the brown cloth strap around his arm he knew was for checking blood pressure.

"How long will I be here?" he said. He wanted her to look at him, but she was concentrating on what she was doing.

"Not long. A day or two perhaps. Long enough to get your strength back."

He smothered a groan. Just a day or two. "I can't stay longer?"

"You might. There's another doctor besides Dr. Sage who needs to see you," she said with no expression, still not looking at him.

Dr. Sage. He'd heard that name before. A young doctor who bought the rundown Rutherford mansion at Cotton Plant and spent a fortune restoring it for his wife who left him the day they moved in. Folks said he had to move into a trailer because of what she did to him in court. "Doc Boswell's my doctor. I don't need two doctors."

"Dr. Boswell's not on staff here. Dr. Sage was on duty when you came in."

That's all he needed, a doctor in worse shape treating him. He watched her hand pump the little black bulb, her eyes blue and still, steady. So kind and gentle, he thought. Some man's lucky to have her. He looked to see. No ring on her finger. The pressure tightened around his arm then stopped. He felt his heart beating under the pressure.

"What other doctor?"

"Now don't talk, Mr. Pasley. Be quiet." The cold stethoscope tingled on his arm. She turned the little knob close to the bulb, and the pressure began dropping, his heartbeat with it. She checked her watch again. His arm went limp. She unwrapped the strap and wrote on the clipboard.

"What other doctor?"

"My, you're a persistent one. A psychologist."

He pushed himself up in the bed. "I'm not seeing any shrink."

"He's not a shrink. His name is Dr. Matthews, and he can help with problems Dr. Sage can't."

He still couldn't make out the look on her face, except that a concern moved there. From a silver pitcher beaded with moisture, she began pouring water into a clear plastic cup. "Here. This'll help." She handed him two purple pills. She was not looking at him but out the window.

"What are these?"

"They're tranquilizers. They'll help you sleep."

His mother had taken nerve pills once, and he remembered what they did to her. "I think I can sleep without them."

"Doctors orders. Now be a good patient and down the hatch."

The cup was cool in his hand, and the water went through his mouth like a gift from God. He swallowed the pills and drained the cup and asked for another.

She poured one more, and he downed it quickly.

"That's enough for right now," she said. "You need to rest. I'll check on you after a while."

"Not long."

"No. Not long," she said with a smile and left.

He'd never taken tranquilizers before and wondered how they'd make him feel. Would he just get dizzy and pass out? Would he feel drunk? Would they make him look and act stupid? He didn't need to say anything stupid. He lay there waiting, thinking again of his children, of Lizzie. Sooner or later, she'd hear. He didn't need to face her. He needed to tell the nurse to put a sign on the door. He didn't want to talk to anybody, except her,

Margie. That was her name. She didn't know all about him. He could talk to somebody who didn't know all about him.

A faint movement was beginning in his head when the door opened and a face peered around it.

"Hap?"

"Rooker. What the hell are you doing here?"

"Just came to check on you."

"How'd you know I was here?"

Rooker stood there, turning the brim of his hat through his fingers. His eyes were red and bleary, like he'd been up all night. He cleared this throat. "Operator notified us when the call came in. Then there was anoth—"

"I'm surprised they let you in here. They told me to rest. Won't even let me talk."

"They didn't. I checked the board at the nurses' station and waited till the coast was clear. 'Sides, ain't nobody gonna stop a deputy of the law." The smile on Rooker's face was twitching in the corners, like it couldn't stay there long, and it didn't. "Knowing what was going on 'tween you and Lizzie and all, I figured somebody needed to tell you, I mean," he cleared his throat again, "somebody you knew and all, somebody in the family needed to know. We didn't know how to contact no other family members 'cept through you . . . and next of kin got to be notified."

The rim of Booker's hat was turning faster through his fingers, and his body was shaking. His face looked almost white against the wall behind him.

"What are you talking about, next of kin? I'm alive, Rooker, not dead." He began to feel a warmth spread through his face.

"Hap." He paused and looked out the window then back at him. "Something awful has happened." His voice was trembling, and he seemed close to tears. "Your mama died just shortly ago."

For a moment, it was as though a great wind swept through him, taking breath and blood and thought with it. Rooker looked far away, unreal, like some dream on the wall that was far away, too, and the words coming from him even further away, a distant whisper. Surely, he didn't hear him right. Surely not. Surely, he'd said something else.

"Wha . . . What?"

Rooker took a step closer toward the end of the bed, his hat still now in his hands, his voice choking. "I said, your mama died just a while ago. Ambulance brought her to the hospital. They did everything they could to bring her back. But they couldn't."

"Oh, no . . . no . . . no . . . not Mama . . . no . . . not Mama . . . " Far away. Everything got far away. Falling through darkness. Nothing to catch. Got to grab something. "Mama . . . no Mama." He gripped the sides of the bed with his hands.

"Sorry, Hap, for having to break it to you like this, but—"

"Just a minute, Rooker . . . can't breathe . . . gotta catch my breath."

"Want me to get a nurse?"

"Yeah . . . no . . . I don't know . . . Mama . . . Mama . . . my Mama. Dead. Gone. My God. Gone." He felt his body sobbing, but no sounds coming out.

"Know how you feel, Hap. Lost mine three year ago. Hurts like hell."

His hands gripped the edges of the mattress tighter, squeezed harder on wads of plastic and blanket and sheet. He held his breath a moment then let it out slowly. A calmness seemed to come in where everything had suddenly left.

"My God. I knew this would kill her. Knew it."

"Wadn't this, Hap."

"What?"

"Wadn't this. I mean . . . you know . . . " Rooker was fumbling with his hat again, his head turning from side to side, up and down, looking into the corners, at the ceiling, then at him. "She didn't have no . . . " His jaw was opening and closing with nothing coming out. "It wadn't no . . . Damn, Hap. I done done it now. Shit. She done it to herself, Hap."

"Done it to herself? You don't mean—"

"Like I said, Hap, hated to break it—"

"Oh, God. No. How could she? How could she?"

"God Almighty, Hap. I didn't mean . . . I shouldn't've . . . " Rooker's chest was heaving. "I'm sorry, Hap."

He caught his breath. "That's okay, Rooker." He swallowed to talk again. "I just need to be alone."

Rooker left. He didn't see him go, just heard the door click. A numbness moved through him. The room looked darker and the night sky lighter through the window. His breathing came from deep inside and sounded loud. He wanted to cry, but there was nobody or nothing to cry to. There was just himself. He could cry to himself, but himself was empty and probably wouldn't hear it. It was as though he was totally alone and pain had nowhere to go but stay and settle, just be. That was the numbness he felt, the no feeling he'd never felt before. He had only himself now. Somehow, it was something to lean on. His eyelids were heavy. The darkness he entered couldn't hurt him anymore.

A hand touched his arm, and he opened his eyes.

"Do you feel up for company?"

She was back. It took a moment to remember who she was and why she was there. She wasn't looking at him but over him.

"Company?" He couldn't tell her.

"Someone's in the lobby. She says she's your wife."

She poured him a cup of water and handed it to him and finally looked at him, a worried look.

"My wife? Here? How'd she know?"

"She said someone at the sheriff's department called her. She's pretty upset. You don't need a lot of excitement and . . . there's been something . . . " He watched her struggle. "You've been through a lot, and Dr. Sage didn't know if you should be . . . She's talked with him . . . but your pulse is strong and your blood pressure back to normal, so maybe it's okay. We just need your permission."

The sudden thought of seeing Lizzie. He couldn't answer. He thought he knew why he feared her seeing him like this. She'd think he did it to get attention, to distract her from Billy Ray and God only knows what else. No one would believe he didn't plan it, that the idea just hit him and it seemed the thing to do to get rid of the pain. She wouldn't believe that, that he saved his own life for his kids, not her. She'd probably heard about his mother and thought it ran in the family. Maybe she wouldn't ask. Maybe she didn't care enough to. She just came because, that too, was the thing to do. He looked out the window and threw a prayer into the lonely night where a quarter-moon cupped a star. It might come back with an answer.

"I can just tell her no, Mr. Pasley, doctor's orders."

"No."

She looked at him like she was waiting for him to say more. "No? You want me to tell her no?"

"No. Yes. I mean, yes. It's okay for her to come in."

He told himself silently to be calm and closed his eyes to say another prayer, this time to himself. A dreamy warmth began to spread upward from his legs and arms, through his chest, into his cheeks and eyes, which he was afraid to open.

22

Hap and Liz

Tall and narrow windows surrounded the empty lobby and Lizzie could see the moon and several stars. Two magazines lay on the small table in front of her—*Women's World* and *Family Circle.* Their covers were torn, edges frayed. They had been there a long time, gone through hundreds of hands that had nothing else to do but wait. He might not be able to have company, they told her, but they would check. They. People in white clothes who walked like they had air under their feet that gave them a special elevation. People with name tags too small to read but acting like they were neons you could see a mile away. People behaving like they knew more than they were letting on, and probably did. He just didn't want to see her. That was probably the reason. She couldn't blame him. After all, she started it, her and her stupid fantasies. Why couldn't she have just kept them in her head, corralled there, instead of opening the gate, riding herd. That way they would've always been hers, always there to look forward to, there in her head at least, almost as real as life. Now there was nothing. No fantasies. No dreams. Folks should be content to just dream. Let a dream out of your head and you kill it, if it doesn't kill you first.

She knew he didn't know, that she'd have to be the one to break the news. She wished she'd called Brother Hammingtree to come with her, but she didn't think of that until now, and now was too late. She'd never done that before, been the first to tell someone a loved one had died. One nurse told her under no circumstances should he be told, another that he was sedated and out of it. That nurse was the one who said the doctor thought this might not be a good time but that there was never a good time, that he was stabilized and being given tranquilizers to help his body absorb the shock. She wanted to ask the doctor for some for herself, but then there probably weren't any pills for guilt. That was a shock a person had to absorb on their own.

A nurse entered the lobby, walking toward her, the same one who told her under no circumstances. She braced herself for more of the same.

"Mrs. Pasley?"

"Yes."

"Your husband said he would see you now. He's still recovering, but he's improving." Her tone was kinder. She noticed her name plate this time. Margie Rather. "We don't know how he's going to handle this. He's still kind of fragile." The world sure does shrink when trouble hits, she thought. Surely, she was no relation.

She followed the nurse down a long hallway then another to a door at the end.

"You can go in," the nurse said. "But we do need to limit your time to ten minutes. We gave him a pretty good dose of tranquilizers."

"Would you mind waiting here outside the door, I may need you."

"Yes, of course. But he may fade on you."

She nodded and pushed on the door.

•   •   •

He heard the soft click of the door shutting and the rustle of movement in the room and opened his eyes. She was standing at the foot of his bed.

"Hap?"

"Yeah?"

"I came to check on you."

"I'm proud you did."

"I had to."

"Had to?"

"Wanted to."

"You didn't have to."

"I know."

Silence lay between them, like something dead that couldn't be shoved aside, wouldn't budge.

They waited each other out.

.   .   .

She stared at the tubing in his arm, followed it up to the sack of blood hanging over him, then to the bandages around his wrists, stalling for time to figure the right words, how to tell him. No way seemed good.

.   .   .

He could barely see her, looking at everything about him, but him. His need for her fought the fear of needing her, fear holding the edge. She'd have to speak first. He couldn't.

Finally, she did. "They said you were lucky."

He looked out the window, thought about that word, lucky, felt heaviness in his eyes, tingling around his lips, thickness swelling his tongue.

"They said that, huh?"

"Yes. They did."

"Who are they, anyway?"

"People who saved your life."

He kept looking out the window into the dark. She didn't know. They just helped. Cleaned and patched him up. He'd have lived anyway. But maybe he was the only one who needed to know that, him and God.

"I'm grateful. Are you? I never expected our issues to come to this."

Why did she say that? What did she expect it to come to? She felt something for him. Not love but not not love. Maybe she'd have felt it for anybody who'd almost died. She saw his head dip and his eyes almost close. Then his head came up and his eyes flared, like a light will before it burns out.

She had to go ahead and get it over with. "Hap, I've got some bad news." She walked over and put a hand on his arm and squeezed gently.

His head was lolling and his eyes rolling.

The words were there, but she couldn't make them come out. They were simple words, if she could just get them out. Seconds. It would just take seconds, then it would be over. She said a prayer to herself then told him, the only way she knew how. "Your mother died this evening." She was just trying to break it gently. God would forgive her that. She was dead on arrival. Suicide. She'd never tell him that and hoped no one else would.

• • •

She was up close but looked far away. She floated closer then away. He could barely hear her. "I know," he said, his own words sounding far away too.

"You know?"

"Yes."

"How?"

"Rooker told me." Her face, the moon, the night behind that, everything was fading, dissolving fast. "Guess the toughest part's . . . ahead."

"The toughest?"

"The woman."

"What woman?" she shrugged. "Your attorney called me, told me she had no case, it's all circumstantial. Memphis Police Department conducted an evaluation. Another man was there before you. The woman has a reputation. Joe Mack threatened to sue her for defamation. She dropped the charges." She smiled.

Her smile. That was the last light he saw as the dark warm covered him.

• • •

A chair was behind her and she pulled it to the bed and sat down. She placed her other hand on his arm and held it, squeezing every now and then, hoping he could at least feel that.

The nurse came in and whispered it was time to go.

"Can't I stay? Just sit and stay? He'll need me when he wakes up."

"No ma'am. He really needs—" The nurse looked at her a long moment then nodded and left.

Through the window, the moon burned bright, its tips upturned. Her mother had always told her that meant fair weather was on its way. She needed her mother to be right, one more time.

The End

ABOUT THE AUTHOR

Joe Edd Morris is the award-winning author of several novels that include *The Lost Page*, *The Lost Gospel*, and *The Devil Walks at Midnight*. Joe Edd's non-fiction theological works include *Ten Things I Wish Jesus Hadn't Said*. His short fiction has appeared in multiple literary journals with a nomination for the Pushcart Prize.

Joe Edd is a psychologist and retired United Methodist minister. He and his wife, Sandi, live in Tupelo, Mississippi where he has a private practice in psychology, enjoys traveling, gardening, playing the piano, and writing.

OTHER TITLES BY JOE EDD MORRIS

FICTION

Land Where My Fathers Died

Inherit the Land

The Will

The Prison

Torched: Summer of '64

The Lost Page

The Lost Gospel

The Devil Walks at Midnight

NON-FICTION

Ten Things I Wish Jesus Hadn't Said

Old Testament Stories: What Do They Say Today?

New Testament Stories: What Do They Say Today?

Revival of the Gnostic Heresy: Fundamentalism

The Christian Right: Neither Christian Nor Right

Jury Selection in Mississippi: A Systematic Approach

NOTE FROM JOE EDD MORRIS

Word-of-mouth is crucial for any author to succeed. If you enjoyed *The Weaning Hill*, please leave a review online—anywhere you are able. Even if it's just a sentence or two. It would make all the difference and would be very much appreciated.

Thanks!
Joe Edd Morris

We hope you enjoyed reading this title from:

www.blackrosewriting.com

Subscribe to our mailing list – *The Rosevine* – and receive **FREE** books, daily
deals, and stay current with news about upcoming
releases and our hottest authors.
Scan the QR code below to sign up.

Already a subscriber? Please accept a sincere thank you for being a fan of
Black Rose Writing authors.

View other Black Rose Writing titles at
www.blackrosewriting.com/books and use promo code
PRINT to receive a **20% discount** when purchasing.